TOTAL ECLIPSE

TOTAL ECLIPSE

Tony Buchsbaum

Doubleday
NEW YORK
1988

This is a work of fiction. All names, places, characters, and incidents are entirely imaginary, or have been used fictitiously. Any resemblance to actual events, or to persons living or dead, is coincidental.

Library of Congress Cataloging in Publication Data

Buchsbaum, Tony, 1961–
Total eclipse.

I. Title.
PS3552.U3324T6 1988 813′.54 87-5332
ISBN 0-385-23979-3

PRINTED IN THE UNITED STATES OF AMERICA
FIRST EDITION

Every boy searches to find a girl who is like his mother. In my case, it's more of a challenge, for lightning strikes in the same way but once. I always did love a challenge.

This book is dedicated to my mother, Jane, who represents, and who taught me, everything I most value.

This book was edited by David Gernert, who took a writer and helped him become an author.
All novices should be so lucky.
David, thank you.

Tony Buchsbaum

ONE

Like a movie, he kept seeing it all before him, in the steam: The drive over to her house, the front door with its trimmed boxwood hedges, the brick steps up to the door, the doorbell—inside the button must have been a tiny bulb, because it shone in the dark—the sound of the bell deep inside the house somewhere, two chime sounds, that was all, and the waiting.

The waiting until she would open the door. The wait for almost five minutes before he rang the bell again. Then the not too startling realization that no one would be answering the door, no one greeting him and maybe even asking him inside for a drink, or to meet her parents, the thought of which now made Jason laugh because, after all, it was their first date, and prior to it, he wasn't sure she even knew he was alive. Meet her parents? He laughed again, then put his face under the fiery jets of water.

Soon he remembered Deed. Deed would be here in ten minutes—he was always on time, Deed was.

Jason took the nearly used bar of soap in his hands and began lathering up. He began at his legs, working slowly upward. When he reached his groin, he skipped to his abdomen, saving the best, he thought, for last. He made circles with the lather on his stomach until he had a sticky, soapy goo there, then he put the wisp of soap back into the dish. He ran his hands over the goo, gathering it up in his palms, spreading it over his chest, up his arms and over his shoulders, around his neck. He adored the smooth track the soap gave his hands; he liked the feel of wet skin against wet skin, especially his own. He ran his hands over his face, closing his eyes tight against the soap; he poked his fingers into his ears, thinking he would get himself especially clean.

Finally, he knew it was time. He slowly ran his hands around his neck, then down across his chest and stomach, down to his groin. He found himself hard, as he always was at this point, and began to stroke, slowly at first, then quicker. He began to pant, knowing that, like always, the panting would bring on excitement, anticipation, especially in the steam. He pumped harder, faster, until it was nearly too late to stop, before he remembered the rope.

The rope hung on a small hook in the cabinet below the sink, hidden away from everyone. He swung the shower door open slowly, noting the drips of water on the rug, the drips his father always complained about. He didn't care this time. He managed to hook the rope on his index finger, drawing it into the shower with him. He carefully wound it around his neck, over the lather still there, a little tighter than usual. The end he tucked into the coils, fashioning a collar. He looked down to see if he was still hard. He was, he saw, and smiled.

For a moment, he imagined her on the floor of the shower, her hands on him, rubbing him the way he liked. But no one could do it the way he did it to himself; no one ever could. He erased her from there.

With his right hand running the length of his hardness,

his left hand slowly and deliberately went to his neck. He smiled as he forced his left thumb under the coils of the rope, behind his neck, making the collar tighter still. He wouldn't have far to go this time, not too far at all. He stroked, panting again, thinking, If it weren't already steamy in here, I'd make it so.

A spasm rammed through him, and he smiled again. His panting became faster in the excitement. He slowly increased the pressure on the collar with his thumb. He felt the coils dig into the skin on his neck, and he knew he would have to wear turtlenecks the rest of the week to hide the bruise marks.

He saw her face on the glass door perfectly. The blond hair, high in a French braid, the green eyes, the mouth he wanted to kiss. He would have, if only they—

—could feel this good, then they'd know what happiness is all about. I know, thought Jason. I know and they never will.

He increased the pumps and the panting, and pulled tighter on the collar. He thought, I'll have to stop the pressure soon, one more pull should do it.

He screamed, a long one. He hadn't ever screamed before.

The pumping became too quick for him to make out his hand, it was just a slippery blur down there. And he pulled the collar again, but harder this time, almost yanking it, still panting. He knew that the pressure on his neck, the absolute danger in pulling on the collar, the intensity would make the moment so much more fulfilling, so much deeper, so—so orgasmic, he thought. He pulled again, loosening the hold he had on control. He had never had it this tight, but he didn't stop it, he kept on pumping, faster and faster, and his mind told him it would be any second now and then he'd be there, and he pulled the collar again and now the muscles in his thumb hurt, he had to rest, just a few more seconds and he'd be fine, just a few, and he pumped it even faster, he didn't know it was possible, and he closed his eyes, and imagined himself thrusting into her again and again and again and he heard her screams of passion, calling his name Jason Jason Jason don't stop don't stop and he didn't stop Jason and he felt the pain in his neck and his heart and he found it hard to pant but he tried harder and felt harder and saw her face Jason Jason don't stop and then, and then, he felt the surge, felt it coming, from deep down inside, the well pushing itself inside out out out, and he heard her panting and saw her smile, the twinkle in her green eyes and as he pulled out of her he pulled on the collar once more, thinking he would show—

Outside, Deed knocked on the door. While he waited for Jason to open it, he watched a kooky breeze cha-cha with a small pile of leaves on the walkway, not two yards from where he was standing. Minutes passed. He said he'd be ready at nine. It was ten after now. Where was he?

Deed knocked again, harder this time. He tried the knob, but it was locked.

"Shit!" he said, and rapped his fist on the door. It swung open.

TWO

I can hear water running, that's all I can hear. Where it's coming from, I don't know. But it's running, I can hear it. And I can see, I can see the blood—

—swirling around in the last bit of water in the shower, its smoky fingers grasping the length of rope while at once losing its battle against the force of the spiral suck of the drain—

—on Jason's face, somehow, choked out, or convulsed, as the life beelined from him—

—on my shirt. The one that fits, the white one. The blood won't wash out, or the stain in me, or the image of his face.

They keep asking me about it, but I don't want to talk. You ask what happened, I say shut up. Period. Just shut the fuck up.

After they take him away, I go walking, nowhere to go. I hear my eyes blinking the whole time, like they're trying to wash the pictures of it away. But it doesn't do any good, the blinking, there's such a pounding. The eyes, it's only the eyes, bright as ever, and his mouth, wide, screaming, broken, nothing about them the same anymore. All I want to do is get Jason's face out, and I can't do it.

I . . . So I look at the faces at the counter in the Grill on Carrollton, where I end up, people stuffing burgers in and trying to juggle babies on their laps while they eat, which I remember my mother trying to do with me sixteen or seventeen years ago.

The walls here are camellia pink, slightly stained by years of burnt grease and dirt in the heavy air. Paintings of flowers are hung high on the walls and a Mickey Mouse clock silently ticks away the days weeks months years. The green leather on the spinning seats matches the green leather on the side benches, where you have to wait until a seat opens. The glass doors on the pie cabinet are cracked, always have been. I close my eyes a second and imagine the look of the place a generation ago, when my folks were my age, when (so my dad says) they served doughnuts cooked and flattened on the grill, toasty brown. And now here I sit, eyes open, in the same place, on the same spinning seat, seeing the same faces, hearing the same sounds which fill up the room, with the same water, using the same cloth napkins. If there's any kind of beauty at all in living here, in this city, this is it, this repetition, this sameness.

From my seat I can see across the street to my old high school. I used to come here to the Grill for lunch. The owner would give me his business cards, which entitled me to free meals. Eventually, after he died, his son took the place over; I wonder if Michael is here tonight, I haven't seen him. I miss his father now.

I think about school, how I hated it, this and my grade school, which isn't here, but somewhere else, ten minutes away, the same school my grandmother went to, and my mother, and my sister, Becky. One year there, I almost didn't go to PE at all. Instead, I went to the audiovisual room. The man there let me tinker with the different projectors. It never really bothered me that I was cutting a class; I didn't think of it like that. Eventually, though, they caught on: One day, the principal was waiting for me in the AV room. He said, "Get back to the field!" I ran home. That night, he called my father, and I knew I'd have to start going the next day. When I did, the coach put me in the locker room, away from the other boys, to clean up the locker area and the weight room. The whole place reeked of sweat and dirt. I hated it, but it was better than being embarrassed outside. When report cards came out, I had a C, somehow. I figured it was the principal, who I kind of thought hated PE when he was a kid, too.

For a while I liked the idea of being the first in my family to leave it. I still remember how shitty all the kids were to the ones who weren't as good at football as they were in, say, math. My grandmother to this day refuses to call Benjamin Franklin High School by its name, using instead the shorter "Booker T." For her, this seems to indicate better the fact that it's a public school.

Harry comes around and places a dressed burger before me, and a plate of extra-crispy fries, a small dish of mayo, and a mocha freeze.

"How you doin', my man?"

"Okay, Harry, how are you?" I ask absently.

"Pretty good, pretty good, can't complain." Harry has been here at the Grill since my mother was fifteen. My dad used to tell me Harry was famous here for talking to all the customers about baseball. Harry knew all the teams, all the scores, everything. Even now, as you're walking out, the last thing you hear is from Harry: "See you at the ballpark."

Harry puts relish and onion tubs in front of me, along with bottles of ketchup and mustard, salt and pepper. I cover the burger with relish and dip a couple of fries into the mayo, and Harry says, "Where's your friend tonight?" and I know he means Jason. I look up at him, thinking maybe it shows. How else could he know already? Does my face look any different? Then I remember the blood on my shirt, but when I look down at it, it's already dried and doesn't look much like blood, thank God, more like (this isn't the night for this kind of thought) ketchup. Finally, I tell him I don't know.

Gary comes in with that girl he's been dating, Sherri. Sherri dots her *i* with a tiny circle, which to me says it all, and I think now how amazing it is that one simple action like that can capsulize a personality forever.

Across the counter and down a little ways, a woman slaps the baby in her lap. There's a spilled Coke all over the Formica. Now the kid wails much louder than he was laughing a moment ago.

There are no seats for Gary and Sherri, so they take places behind me on the bench. One couple is ahead of them. I look over and smile at Gary, then make a face when Sherri's head is turned. Gary knows what I'm saying: He's not dating her, he's fucking her. It's no big deal, because Sherri's been the watering hole for the class since freshman year. Besides, for her, Gary's just another month or two on the calendar. I steal a few glances over there as I manage to get to the burger finally and remember back a few years ago, when Gary's skin was like a pizza with the works. Sherri sure helped clear it up for him: the finishing touch.

I give up on the burger, no appetite, but draw what's left of the freeze through the straw and stand up, pulling the menu slip out from under the salt shaker, like some magician I once saw who pulled a tablecloth off a fully set table without toppling a single glass. But the salt shaker goes flying over the inside edge of the counter, and I remember that this hasn't been a day I will want to remember, anyway.

"See you," Harry says, "at the ballpark."

After I pay, I go back over there to chat a minute with Gary, and when I get there, he says, "We were over at AT Two's and Barbara was there with some guy from De LaSalle. I thought Jason had her tonight," and all I want to do is hit him across the face, but I don't. All I can do is say, "Yeah, I dunno . . ." and walk away, out into the dark.

I walk around the corner for some coffee, but Häagen-Dazs is closed early tonight. So I walk up Carrollton toward Marian's.

The first time I saw Marian I was at a pizza place on Magazine. She looked at me, and I looked at her, simple as that. Also, Phil Collins was on the stereo somewhere. I had three slices of pepperoni with green peppers and extra cheese, and I was alone because Chip was still hung over from the night before at Cooter's. Marian was at the back with another girl, who wasn't very pretty, and when I caught her eye I smiled. She looked away, then back.

When she finished and left with the girl, I followed them. They split and Marian went home, so I knew where she lived. Before the door swung closed, I said hi.

"What are you doing here?" she said.

I didn't know what to say, because how do you tell someone you followed her home, so I just said I wanted to meet her. I said then, "I didn't know any other way to do it."

"I don't like being followed," she said. She tossed her Alabama-red hair back.

"I'm sorry. I don't do it a lot."

"I hope not," she said, and tossed again.

"I'll never follow you again, I promise." I crossed my heart. "What's your name?"

"I'm not sure I want to tell you. . . . What's yours?"

"Deed Smith. C'mon, I won't bite." I smiled my best I-won't-bite smile.

She looked around, a streetcar rolled by behind me, blew the breeze around. "Pity," she said softly, and I could just hear her over the sound of the streetcar.

Her face was one big pout. Very sexy, I thought. It's like it started with her lips, very puckered and full, and went on from there, spreading innocently out like the circles in a pool after you drop a stone in. *Very* sexy. She still wouldn't look at me. "Marian McMillan," then. "Now you know."

"Now I know. Nice to meet you," I said, putting my hand out. I knew this was a girl I wanted to touch. She didn't take it, though, she just tossed her hair again.

"So now that you know, what do you want?"

"You wanna go out sometime?" I said.

"Where?"

"I don't know yet."

"Maybe," she said, smiling a little. "I'll have to think about it."

I started to say something, but before I did, she turned and went inside and closed the door. Through the glass I saw her walk up the stairs and go through another door at the top. That walk, I thought, and almost knocked on the door; then I almost pounded, but when I finally walked across to the streetcar stop, I hadn't done anything.

A few days later I was at the Grill with Jason. It smelled funny, like burnt beef. It was crowded, too, and we had to wait for seats. We waited for Harry. After we sat down, Jason ordered a junior club sandwich, fries, and a mocha freeze. I saw Michael near the kitchen door and waved to him. He lifted his chin in response, and I ordered a burger, fries, and a Coke.

"Junior club on wheat toast, burger with a dress on, two

orders of fries," Harry said to the chef, a tall black man with a standing white hat on his head.

With his club, Jason got a small dish of mayo. Before each bite, he coated the edge with it. And we both dipped our fries into it, something we saw some guy do here a few years ago. He was across from us, dunking his fries into this dish of mayo. Some girl near us wearing a Tulane sweatshirt asked him what he was doing, if it was good, and he offered her one. She took it, then ordered her own. The next time Jase and I were in, we got it, too.

After dinner, I wanted banana cream pie, but Jason wanted Häagen-Dazs around the corner. I went with him. Behind the counter was Marian, in a loose red shirt that said "STRAWBERRY" in white capitals on the back. She stopped dead when she saw me. I said hi.

"Hi," she said. "Did you follow me *here,* too?"

"I thought I said I'd never follow you again," I said.

"Yeah, I know, but . . . Anyway—"

"Can I have a taste," Jason interrupted, "of chocolate chocolate chip?"

"Sure," Marian said, tossing her hair, and scooped a bit onto a tiny white spoon.

I asked her how she was.

She looked at me. "Fine."

"You busy this weekend?"

"I—"

"Okay," Jason said, "I'll have two scoops of coffee in a waffle cone."

I looked at Jason. He smiled at me. Marian scooped it up.

"Well?" I said when she was done.

"I don't have any plans yet for this weekend," she said.

"How about a movie, and dinner or something?"

She handed Jason the cone and told him how much.

After she gave him his change, she said, "I don't know yet what I'm doing this weekend."

"What does that mean?"

"What?" she said.

"Does that mean yes, or no?" I looked her in the eye; I hate being jerked around.

"It *means* I don't know what I'm doing yet."

"Well," I said. "Today's Monday. If you say yes, that you'll go out with me, then you'll know all week what you'll be doing this weekend. If you wait, then you'll just make other plans and say no eventually. Or I might make other plans."

She looked at me over the sorbets, her eyes thin. "Look, I don't like being manipulated."

"Yeah. Me neither." Then I said, "Come on, Jason, this is a blow," and turned away.

We went out and back around to sit on one of the green cast-iron benches in front of the Grill. After a while, Marian came along, spotted us sitting there watching the world go by.

"Hey, Deed," she said to get my attention, because she didn't know she already had it.

"Yeah," I said, not moving, not looking at her.

"Let's go out Friday night, okay?"

"You sure you want to? I don't want to fuck up your other plans."

"I want to. I'm sorry," she said.

"Okay. But Saturday. I'm busy Friday. I'll pick you up at seven," I said. Jason was almost done. Feeling shit-kicking cool, I looked over at Marian, but she had already started back around.

No one answers at Marian's, so I walk for a while, maybe an hour, and end up at Cooter Brown's, near the Grill. The place is packed, and there's this cloudy cover from the ceiling to where my nose comes, very convenient. Most everybody is sitting at the wooden cafeteria-style tables or in booths. And most everybody has a beer. The walls are covered with license plates from all over the country; under them is a mustardy kind of yellow. Jason once told me his grandfather had teeth the color of these walls.

Richard is there, in the back room where the tables are, taking a pair of kids for quarters. I get a beer from the bar and go back there to watch. Richard lets them sink a few balls on him, and then as I get there he looks at me and winks a hello, then goes to it. He quickly sinks all the rest of his stripes, then the eight. The kids walk away, and he hands me a cue as I walk over.

"Deed," he says. Richard isn't big on talking, never was, which for tonight is jake by me. I can smell pot on his breath even with just that one syllable, and I can see the color of the whites of his eyes—yellow, and not far from the shade on the walls. But he's alert and on top of the game if nothing else.

Silent, he racks them up and breaks, sinking two solids. After another falls, he misses, and I line up a shot to the corner, an easy shot he's left me. I miss it.

I take a few swallows of the beer without tasting it, and it feels good so cold in my throat, and Richard takes care of the rest of the table, sinking all his solids, then all my stripes without a hitch. The table's still his.

"You okay, man?" he asks.

I nod something, knowing he'll interpret it in some way which doesn't matter at all, not tonight, and probably not tomorrow.

A couple walks up to the table, and the guy asks Richard if he wants to play, which is about the same thing as asking a goldfish if he'd like to stay in the bowl. They are on a date, this guy and girl, and Richard says he will, and racks them up again. The girl is wearing a canary-yellow leotard and a tight black satin miniskirt, sort of preppy, sort of punk. No-sense outfit. The guy's hair is gelled and messy. He's got on a flannel shirt, untucked, and jeans, dirty, and loafers, no socks. Figures.

Richard breaks and a stripe falls. He misses the next, and the guy takes over. He lines up a shot across the table, leans over, and the girl stands directly behind the pocket, her crotch at the edge of the table. No way a guy can miss that shot, not with that aim.

I go back out to the bar, where I see some people I used to know over in a tiny corner booth, laughing. An old Donna Summer thing comes on the stereo, and I think that's as good a time as any to get out of there.

Outside, I see a friend of Becky's bending over her car, throwing up. I can't stop looking at her, not until I turn the corner and lose sight altogether.

I walk over to Franklin and think about all the shits I went to high school with. The first building on the far side is where I had art every morning of high school life. Art was the best because I could do anything and it was still art. The pencils, the canvases, the paints—they were enough therapy to get me through. When there's a male teacher who wears makeup every day, with jet-black hair done up in a do, you need something. (One day I was with Chip, and we saw the man on the street. Chip got a good look at him and said, "That man scares me.")

On the sidewalk an old, faded report card blows around in the wind. In ninth and tenth grades I spent half my time forging those things. They had us fill in our names and class names, so all the teachers had to do was fill in the grade and sign it. After a few "Can I have another? I lost mine" lines, I had collected maybe a dozen blanks. Giving myself the make-the-grade grades was a snap; forging the signatures of the teachers was the bitch, but I handled it fine, no sweat. What I thought was a card on the sidewalk blows around, and it turns out to be just a piece of notebook paper.

The grades would make my dad really happy for about a day, which was about all I could expect, because that's the way it was, and he'd tell me, "Walt, that's good work, I'm proud of you," but I never bought it, maybe because as good as it felt, it also felt like shit because of the guilt. For all the crap he gave us, Dad was Dad, and losing Mom was still a bitch to handle sometimes. For him, especially, when he was reminded of her by Becky and me.

Later, when my grades were good all by themselves, he said nothing. By then we'd pretty much stopped talking because of Frankie, and there was too much shit in the way all the time, between my mouth and his ear. I did everything I could to bait him, to provoke him, to push him as far as possible. I think I wanted to break him, like some kind of toy. At night I used to thank God, or whatever, that I'd left Newman to go to Franklin, simply because it was public and very free, and any way I could get out of that bastard's pocket, the happier I knew I'd be. Hell, the reason my grades got better was only so I could stop bothering to lie about them to make him happy, or proud. Shit.

By the time it got to that, though, Frankie was no longer a part of my life; the times I spent thinking about her were the times I spent sending her to the darkest, hottest corners of hell. Holding my father's hand.

Around the back of Franklin, the gate is open and I go in. The annex rooms are empty and dark. I pass the room I had most lunches in, the room where the lady taught Latin to the real brains. All around me every day were the losers who knew by heart all the tables of contents to every *Starlog* published. But they didn't judge me, didn't push me away, didn't call me "faggot," didn't do much of anything the real guys did. I smile now, thinking their enthusiasm is what made me the sci-fi addict I am now. But where was Jason then . . . ?

All the doors are locked. Through the front windows I can see the trophy case in the hall. And the office. And down the hall, the first lockers, and the science rooms. I remember clearly the terrorized look on the nearly formed faces of the embryonic pigs we dissected. Abortions for the sake of public school biology.

I try to decide whether to walk or jump on the streetcar for home. While I'm making up my mind, I go back to Cooter's for darts. I get another beer and trade my driver's license for three blue darts. I throw a few rounds, badly, before some girl walks up and asks if I want to play. I'm game, and she's pretty enough, so I say, "Sure." She takes the darts and throws. Two drop to the floor, one sticks in the double section of the one-point slice.

I miss altogether.

She racks up another six points on the two: one dart in the double and two singles. She increases her lead every round, until at thirteen I call it a night.

"You're leaving?" she asks.

"Yeah, gotta get out of here," I try to say.

"You want some company?"

I look over at her, to look at her, and she's really not bad, blond hair, with pink leotards and tennis shoes on. Her white blouse is unbuttoned low enough so I can see there's no bra. She's thin, maybe too thin, but thin is for me, and I like the way her tits bounce under the shirt. I say, "Sure."

Walking on St. Charles, she takes out a joint and lights up. She pulls a drag, then offers it to me. I gladly inhale a mean one, then cough half of it away. It's strong weed.

"Good pot, eh?" she says.

"Shit!" I say.

She laughs, takes another hit.

By the time we reach Broadway, we're staggering. She says, "Hey, I live down there." She points in the direction of the river. "My dad's there doing some X with his girl, he said I could bring a friend if I wanted."

"What's X?" I ask.

"You know. XTC."

"Oh," I say.

"It's great. We throw all the pillows in the house all over the floor in the living room, then we cover it all with sheets, then we take off all our clothes and get under the covers and *talk* to each other." She sounds thrilled about it, and I am intrigued for a moment, fascinated.

"That's all?"

"And then we fuck, of course." She smiles. "By the time the X gets in, you don't know who you're fucking, but it's funny because you *do* know who you're talking to."

"Oh."

"So you wanna come and try it?" she asks.

"No," I say. "Not tonight, maybe another time, okay?"

"Sure, sure. I'm at Coot's just about every night. I've seen you in there before," she says, taking my hand. Hers is wet, sticky.

"Yeah, I go . . . sometimes."

She steps closer to me and I think she might kiss me. This close, I can smell the beer and pot in her breath, so convincing that I can almost taste it. Then she steps away. She smiles for a second, then says, "Night. See you 'round, okay?"

"Okay," I say.

I watch her walk, and when she's gone in the dark, I start for home. It's late, past two now, a long time after. It's quiet on the avenue. Not many cars. A couple of streetcars, one going in each direction. The trees, they . . . it's like they're singing, singing softly. It's weird. I don't like it out here now. It's so . . . too lonely. Too quiet. Jason's face floats just ahead of me, his eyes . . . and his mouth. I remember we used to be out this late sometimes, around here, doing exactly this, when he spent a night at my house. Suddenly, I realize the only place he'll ever spend a night again is in my memory. I stop a moment and breathe. He's so far away, and I'm left empty. Shit, even the air is . . . can air be transparent? The walking is slow, a necessary burden. I get about ten yards before I hear yelling across St. Charles Avenue, right outside the dark Katz and Besthoff on the corner. It's three boys running around, laughing and yelling. They each have a can of shaving cream, and when I turn around, two are shaking theirs and one is spraying them with his. The two white-headed blobs huddle a moment, then chase the third boy down the street toward the park. I walk on, with sounds of laughter and spraying shaving cream filling the empty spaces between the rumble of the streetcars.

THREE

I get to the Metronome around ten. Rich has counted my drawer for me because it should be done before ten, so all I have to do is get behind the register and wait. The store seems darker this morning, but it's dark anyway, all the time. The walls are either brick or black, mostly black. And the record bins are chrome, which tends to reflect the black. The big screen of the projection TV is high, beneath the shadow of an overhang, and it's not terribly interesting to watch because the sound is always off.

Two high-schoolers come in right away and get the latest double-Duran album on sale, and the latest Madonna twelve-inch. I ring them up, trying to be cheerful.

Rich puts something on the stereo, something jazz, one of the things he always plays in the morning. I play with the cable box until I find MTV and there's a Benatar video on, one of her better ones if that's possible, but the sound is off, so we can't hear it. Benatar jazzing; it makes no sense, but it's the Metro-norm, so we endure. By the day's end, I have rung up about a grand on a double shift, and I go up to the manager's office to count it up and balance the drawer, which at the beginning was a chore and impossible, but which now is a totally mindless act.

When I get back downstairs, Chip is there already, a few minutes early. Chip's an actor and a writer; he writes about New Orleans and its odd (very odd) ways. It's a decadent place, in my mind, but Chip adores every crack in every sidewalk. He knows how I feel about being here (I refuse to call it "living here"), about having never been farther away than Destin; he endures my calling it nothing but Dixieland.

Chip is one of the best people I know, though I think if he knew I thought it—or said it to anyone—he'd kill me. We met on a streetcar on a hot, crowded Saturday afternoon. He was parked in the last seat, at the back of the car, the driver's seat which faces the rear and which is used only when the streetcar turns around at Claiborne Avenue. His feet were up on the sill, in Siders (his generic name for anything but sneakers), and he had earphones on, the volume up so high I could hear the stuff even over the streetcar noises. What struck me was that it wasn't the Heads, or the Stones, or Scritti, but something smooth, calm, something very—something very Chip.

What it was, was McCoy Tyner, who Chip calls "the coolest." He played with John Coltrane for a while, then went solo. Chip says Tyner's piano is unbeatable, like Wynton Marsalis on trumpet. (When I told Chip that Wynton went to the same high school as I did, he nearly died.) I've heard Tyner since that day, and I think Chip's right. His new disc, "Just Feelin," came into the Metronome last summer, and I played it every day for weeks.

Anyway, that day on the streetcar, Chip had on his 'phones, and I just stood there next to him and listened. Eventually, Chip spun around on the seat and that was that. We met.

Chip is the great-grandson of slaves, from Texas. The way he tells it, somewhere along the line, a couple of white masters fucked a couple of slave women, and the white men's genes passed through, down the generations, to Chip, which explains why his skin is so light, actually the color of coffee with two and a half dashes of cream. (Once, at Café du Monde, we played with a cup of coffee and chicory until we got the color just right.) In all the time I've lived here in Dixieland, I never met anyone with skin the color of Chip's.

His face is the clue to his history-book family tree. His nose is thin, like someone cut it from wood. And his eyes, very blue, with the longest lashes ever. When Chip smiles, you *know* he's happy—if I had his teeth, I'd be that happy, too. And his laugh cuts the noises out of any room, the way it booms and overflows from deep in his throat.

I think one reason I liked him so much, right from the moment I saw him, was his hands. When I first spotted him, his hands were behind his head, fingers woven like a net, relaxed. His fingers are long and thin, like you could easily snap them in two if you wanted. But at the same time, they have something about them, the kind of thing you'd expect to find in his eyes, and you might in someone else's. It's their intensity. Intense fingers.

What draws me to them is that they're a lot like mine. And like my mom's.

If there was one thing about Chip I'd change, it'd have to be this drug thing of his. Every now and then he's really cooked, and I worry. Sure, I've done it a few times—okay, more than a few, but who hasn't? But when I did it Chip was with me. It's when he's alone and does it, I know he lets loose and it's harder to stop, and I know that because he's told me. With me, there's a limit, but with him—I don't think he has one. At least, not anymore. And that scares me. It's like sometimes I wait for him not to show up again. One time we talked it over, after I went off it, off the coke, and after, he didn't talk to me for a while; it didn't go well. So I don't ask him anymore. Besides, he tells me, he writes better stoned.

"Bullshit" is what I say to that, and he knows it, because I've read some of his stuff about Dixieland. He writes what he sees, only he must see something I don't, because somewhere between his blue eyes and his intense fingers, it changes. Somehow, he makes this place sound bearable, I won't say beautiful, but . . . easier.

Though Chip has never met Jason, I always thought they should. Whenever I suggested it, Chip said he had something else to do. The more I think about him, the better I get at figuring him out. I've never seen him with anyone else, never seen anyone he knows, and he never talks about anyone. What I think about Chip is that he's the kind of guy who has to encounter the world one person at a time.

I'm not.

Now, with Jason dead, I wonder. When we're all in heaven, or wherever, and when all the columns are added up, who's going to end up with the better life? Chip, one at a time, and pretty happy? Or me, Deed, with not quite what I want, and not really knowing what I want in the first place, with too many memories and an unsure future, and a girl I don't love who—if she had one wish—would wish for me to.

What I do know is that if *I* had a wish, I'd wish for the answer to that question.

We take his black Mustang down to the Quarter and park on the street somewhere near Canal. On Royal, we stop at Gilmore's so Chip can pick up the new issue of some gay rag, and I catch a glimpse of the cover, which instantly produces a horrible taste in my throat.

We walk one block over to Bourbon and there aren't too many tourists now, but enough. A few people turn their heads to look at the two of us, a tall black guy who looks like a model, and me, looking pretty normal, and very white. Their looks say it all, even on Bourbon, and I dismiss them like I always do. Chip hates them, the tourists, he says, because they pollute his sense of the city's purity, its character, its potential for material, but I think for the most part they're great, Parasites all. Feeding on Dixieland Decadence. I love it.

About three or four blocks in, we stop at a strip joint and stand on the street to watch. The place has men and women together, and the barker stands near the door, swinging it in and out all night, teasing the strollers. If nothing else, it gets us inside, even though I have heard that many of the women on Bourbon Street are only men with partial sex changes.

We pay the cover and order four beers, the minimum. The place has dark, black walls. All the lights are pointed at the stage, where there's a very thin woman with black lace panties and bra on. Neither hides much. She looks stoned. There's music coming from somewhere, some funk crap. After a few minutes, a man comes onstage holding a bullwhip, and the music changes to "Tangerine Dream," stuff from the sound track from *Risky Business,* and for the first time I notice that train tracks are painted on the stage, I guess referring to the movie. Moving with the music, the man removes all his clothes except for his jock, which is also black. I look over at Chip, and he's trying to catch the guy's eyes, and I look back to the stage and see that he has, momentarily. I notice that both the man and the woman are greased, and totally hairless. The man sort of struts over to the woman and rubs his hands over her torso, over her lace bra. He is standing behind her, the bullwhip around her neck, and his other hand clutches at her panties. She seems to writhe under his touch. A strobe comes on, and I catch Chip recrossing his legs. The man unhooks the woman's bra, and it falls away, revealing completely a set of huge tits, and he pulls her panties down to the floor, so she can step out of them. She is shaven and sweaty, as he is; they both shine as if polished. She turns to him, and he laces the bullwhip between her legs, up to her cunt, and when he pulls it back and forth, it is wet, slick, glistening. She no longer appears stoned, and, moaning, they begin to move together as the music reaches its peak. The strobe makes it all seem unreal, and it must be, because they are gone in a moment, and the stage is dark, and the music has stopped.

Chip says, "Let's get out of here," and we leave, back to the street.

We pass one joint which has a woman's legs coming out of the window on a swing, teasing us into that one, too. But we walk on. We turn onto St. Peter and go a little ways, past Preservation Hall, where a couple dozen Parasites are lined up, waiting for the next show to begin. Steps further is Pat O's. There's a line there, too, but we walk past it and into the courtyard, to a table for two. A green-jacketed waiter comes by, tossing two cardboard coasters onto the glass-topped table, and we order two 'Canes. It's crowded, and there's a group of drunk collegers over on the other side of the patio, singing something loudly out of key. I see at least a dozen Hurricane glasses on their table, and a Rainbow, half gone. One girl is fast asleep, her head in a sticky, red puddle on the flooded table.

The whole place is in a courtyard, surrounded by two- and three-floor French Quarter houses. Ivy clings to the brick walls everywhere, and the scene makes me think of Tennessee Williams, some play of his I read in English, I guess. Top 40 crap floods out of the bar, into the courtyard, but I can hear jazz coming from somewhere, maybe Preservation Hall. There's a fountain in the center, a fountain with fire coming out at the top. Firewater, makes sense. Soon I am hypnotized by it.

The Hurricanes come. Chip pays for both, and I don't try to stop him. He lifts his glass to toast, and I match him. "To sex and drugs," he says. He touches his glass to mine, and we drink.

"What about rock and roll?" I ask.

After he downs half in one gulp, he shrugs, then eats the slice of orange from the edge of the glass.

I ask him if he's afraid to die.

"Die? No, man, no. Why do you ask that?"

"I've just been thinking, that's all," I say.

"I guess, but it doesn't bother me." Chip's not looking at me. He's looking everywhere *but* at me, it seems. Is he afraid? Should I reverse all his answers?

"Why not?"

"I never think about it. There's too much else—"

From out of nowhere, two chicks walk up to the table. One is pretty (blond, smallish nose, playful smile), the other isn't (overweight, pasty skin, too long hair), not at all. They speak French to us, which I can't understand and I don't think Chip can, either. Somehow we carry on a conversation in two languages and with a lot of hand signals, neither side really understanding the other. But they pull up chairs and sit with us and laugh. After a while I begin to think maybe these chicks aren't from France at all, probably from Metairie.

I hold up a finger to mean "just a minute," and I say it, and they look perplexed, right on cue, looking at each other and rolling their eyes. I lean over and whisper into Chip's ear. He turns back to the girls and takes the pretty one's hand.

"My friend and I would like to take you back to our place," he says, "and tear off all your clothes and slap our dicks between your tits and then fuck you everywhere possible."

The chicks stop talking, and it's so quiet all of a sudden that I can hear the dribbling of the water in the fountain, and even the flames licking at the air, and the chicks look at each other again, right on cue. Then the pretty one slaps Chip across his face, and we start to laugh. They must leave, because when we open our eyes again, recovering, they are gone.

I look around, and everything's the same. The flames in the fountain kissing the air, the water dropping like rain to the brass bowl below. The people, the drinks, the noise. When I pull my eyes over to Chip, I see he's looking around, too.

"You done?" I ask.

Chip looks at his glass, its girlish curves still half full, half red. It looks swollen. He removes the straw and downs the last of it, just like that. "Yeah."

I get up and walk back toward the entrance, toward St. Peter. I have taken my glass from the table, like any old Parasite. Hell, I *paid* for the thing, may as well add it to the collection. At the door, some green-vested guy pours the rest of my drink into a large plastic-coated cup, and slips the *Playboy*-figured glass into a cardboard holder. On the glass, on the cup, on the holder, is the notorious Pat O'Brien's motto: "Have Fun!" We walk back the way we came, past the joints, past the clubs, and the music and the skin and the smells of long-open liquor bottles and beer, back to the car.

Before we take off, Chip lights up a joint and offers it to me. Despite many promises to myself, I take a hit, then another. When he offers it again, I don't take any. Chip's pot is strong, two hits are plenty.

At home, when I slip the key into the back door, I remember that Jason's funeral was today. My hand on the sliver of brass, I force myself to keep the word "forgot" from entering my thoughts. I rationalize myself away from it altogether, telling myself that the shock of finding him kept me away, kept the thought of the funeral away. I couldn't have forgotten; my brain just didn't allow me to remember. I stand there like a petrified version of myself, eyes straight ahead. Then I blink once and that does it. I close the door behind me and dead-bolt it and lean back against the refrigerator and weep.

FOUR

I feel sick when I wake up. It must be the pot from last night, maybe a bad weed or something. Once I make up my mind to do something, next time I'm going to do it. I knew I shouldn't have taken the hits I did, or the ones later. I've never had this reaction before. One thing I hate about myself when I'm with Chip is my inability to say no, sometimes.

After the usual-type day at work, I go over to Marian's, over on Carrollton, not far from the Grill. While I'm walking over there I remember seeing her that first time at Häagen-Dazs. I think about the night we were in her apartment and I got up and went to the kitchen looking for marshmallow topping. But I found some chocolate sauce in an old Dennery's bottle. So while Marian was in the shower, I warmed it up in a pan and then poured it into a three-cup container thing. When she got back into bed, I threw off the sheet and started dribbling the warm sauce all over her. When she was fairly covered, and long horny, I licked it off her.

We have dinner at Popeye's, which is practically next door to her apartment. It's not as good as usual, maybe because my mind isn't on fried chicken, but on chocolate sauce.

In the middle of a wing, I spot her looking at me in some different way, and it hits me she's thinking of Jason. She asks if I'm okay about it. I tell her I am.

After, we go to Forty-one Forty-one, on St. Charles, in her Beetle. I get a couple of beers. They're playing disco tonight, which I hate, but I dance anyway because I like to, and Marian is great. She smiles a lot, and like always, I think maybe she wants something I'm not ready to give, like a commitment. I smile back an innocent smile, or maybe ignorant.

Back at her place after one, she's a wild woman, and I think about the man and the woman onstage in the Quarter, under the strobe. When it's over, Marian's face is one big smile; I must have done something right. Wherever I touch her tonight, it's magic, and sometimes she shivers when I just go near her. Still, after we're done, uppermost in my mind is *leaving,* not talking. Her eyes do their wordless pleading thing, and I stay a little longer as if I wanted to, lying there lying.

It's been—what?—a year now, and it's going downhill faster than it went up, and that was fast. Pretty pathetic, really. She's become so pitiful in the past couple of months. In her eyes I see that she wants to hear that I love her. At the beginning, I guess I thought I might, but now there's no chance. But how do you *tell* someone that? That after a year of closeness, after a year of sex, after a year of growth, there's nothing but an enormous nothing between you. As fun as Marian can be sometimes, she's a real drag the others. Her dependence on me is too heavy, and I feel claustrophobic.

Soon, lying there, I feel the familiar pressure from her. It grows quickly and I feel crushed by it, until it becomes unbearable, so I leave and take the streetcar home. In the back there is a woman in her forties, drunk, asleep, snoring. At her feet there's a full shopping bag, under her head a holed sweater.

There was this night, a while ago, a couple of years, right after school ended, tenth grade, when we were sixteen. Jason's folks were out of town, and I was staying at his house the weekend of his birthday, and it was late, and it was raining, pouring. At like two-thirty in the morning, he jumped up and grabbed the keys.

Outside, the wind took the rain and threw it at us. It pelted our short-sleeved skin and stung for a second. Just as the first sting faded away, it was replaced by another, and another.

"What are you doing?" I yelled at him. It was hard for him to hear since the wind was blowing so hard, but I had to ask. In front of the house, on the street, was his father's Olds convertible, the top down.

"Shit!" he said. The sun had been hot as hell all day and, as usual, it clouded over late in the afternoon. In all the excitement of the videotape we rented, some X-rated thing from Sidney's, we forgot to put the top up.

By the time we got to the car, we were soaked through to our skin, and the car had inches of water in it, nearly a foot, like a small swimming pool. I saw Jason's face, and though he looked like he knew he'd catch shit, he somehow looked okay, like he'd handle it. There was a smile on his face, that smile that told me Jason had an idea, some strange, sinister idea.

He was wearing his old pink oxford-cloth shirt with the ripped collar and Top Siders. We stood there and stared at the car for a few moments, then he threw his head back and laughed. The wind swirled mist and rain all around us, and a bolt of lightning lit up the night sky and every drop between the clouds and Jason and me. All I could think of was how good it felt to stand there like that, sopping wet, with him. It was like there was a good reason to be there, yet no reason at all. Just the fun of it. It felt . . . free. I couldn't help laughing out loud.

In the lamplight, we seemed to glisten, still pelted by the hail-hard drops of driven rain. Giggling, he and I looked at each other, and I knew if anyone drove by, that would be the end of us forever. They'd surely lock us away. All at once, as we collapsed into hysterical laughter, I put my hand out in his direction, and as lightning flashed over us, he took it in a hard handshake. There was a clap of thunder then, all around, everywhere, and another burst surrounded us with light. It was a startling moment, and after it passed, Jason and I knew there wasn't anything that could tear us apart, that could split our bond. Tonight was like some sort of glue, I don't know.

Then, suddenly, he looked at me. A trace of that Jason smile was there, then gone again, and he said, "Come on!" He jumped into the driver's seat, and I went around to the other side. We displaced gallons, and the water rose closer to the edge of the car, some of it spilling over onto the street. He bent himself into some contortionist's shape and wrestled his keys out of his jeans pocket. He started the car, and we were off to God-knew-where.

In about ten minutes, we were on the highway, I-10, doing something insane, like eighty at least. The downpour hadn't slackened even a little, and now the slight stings were bursts of pain. I'd taken my sneakers off, using one toe to pry the other, then my bare toes to convince its mate away, and I pressed my bare feet, still under water, against the floor of the front seat. The wipers were going, but didn't do much good. I looked over at Jason, and he was laughing just like before, and, when I took a second to notice it, so was I.

"You ready?" he screamed at me.

"For what?" I screamed back, though I didn't care.

Then he did it, he pushed his foot as far down on the gas as it would go. I couldn't see it, but I felt the car shudder forward, and the highway lamps flashed by, and I thought of Han Solo and Luke Skywalker in the *Millennium Falcon,* blasting into hyperspace, when all the stars become strands of light, stretching into infinity.

On the windshield, the rain began to clear away, pushed by the force of the wind coming at us better than a hundred miles an hour. We passed the Causeway exit, and I spotted the tall lights in the parking lot at Lakeside.

I followed the slithering path of the water drops racing up the windshield to the edge, where they joined what had become a sheet of water over us, where the canvas top should have been. Millions of drops, joined in a single arc, acting now as the roof of the car. I saw then that it was no longer raining inside the car. The weather was held outside by the wall of wind and rain. The streams above reflected the sky overhead, turning it into some twisted nightmare, wonderful and absolutely stunning. A totally unexpected phenomenon. Through the windshield, I saw the Clearview exit whiz by. Jason's face was still stretched wide in a smile the size of Texas.

"Do you see this?" I said.

He looked around then, and said, "Yeah. Yeah."

"It's really something, Jase. Really something."

"It's so beautiful. Isn't it?"

I reached up and put my arm through the sheet of water. The chill was startling, surrounding my arm at the wrist line, separating my hand from the rest, making it an undulating, five-pronged mass on the other side.

Jason looked at me, and I smiled at him. It was a moment I knew I'd always carry with me. We were like one person then. All at once, we were screaming, and I felt the car slow a bit. The red needle of the speedometer moved to the left, toward zero. At the Williams Boulevard exit, we turned around and got back on the highway, heading the other way, at a normal speed.

It took about twenty minutes to get back to the house. Climbing out of the car, we looked at each other, at our soaked bodies, and we knew we'd had a night like no one else ever had. I don't think either of us had the words to express it, but we knew *something* had happened. I stood there, taking the event in, then began to walk toward the house.

"Wait," he said, and came around to meet me on my side of the car. The rain had let up a bit; now it was like a gentle spring shower. He walked over to me and put his arms around me, pressing his whole body against mine. It was invigorating to have him against me like that. It was wild, that's what it was. There was no describing it, there was no category for it. It was just a feeling, a force. We were friends. We were brothers. We were everything. Too much, yet not enough. It was the way it should be. That was the way it always was after that, from that night, until the night I found him dead.

In my bedroom, I look out the window, down to the street, and I can just about see us out there in the rain. Drops of water hit the pane then, and it's all washed away. I close my eyes and I feel the warm surge of tears on my face. Jason . . . God, I love you. I loved you. I miss you.

Later, I play with the shells I used to find on the beach in Destin, during summers a long time ago. We used to go every summer for a while, before my mom died, and one year after. I was the kind of boy who got black in one or two days. The water there was deep blue and green, and the sand was like sugar, white-white. From the bridge from Fort Walton Beach into Destin, the view was gorgeous, the white and blue and green spread below. Destin was the best. There were four or five families, and we all went together every year and stayed in small cabins in a place called the Riviera. Some years, we used to be on the beach from before lunch until maybe five-thirty, when the lifeguards would come around and fold up the enormous blue umbrellas, and someone would always bring a special drink for all of us, even the kids. Like, once we did a watermelon which my dad filled with vodka for three days, I think. Or coladas, when they were in. One summer my dad bought me a kite that looked like an enormous bat, with Day-Glo pink eyes stuck on. Destin's beach had a pretty constant breeze, so flying the bat was a snap. That was the best summer, until one day the string snapped, and the bat flew off. Dad ran down the beach after it, but never did get it.

I used to spend days pretending I was James Bond. I'd pretend the water-skiers were the enemy agents, and with my mask and fins (jet-propelled) I could outswim any bullet or spear. The summer Becky was stung by a jelly-fish, we pretty much stayed out of the water, so my dad buried me one day up to my neck in the sand. He took a picture, and I looked like someone had cut my head off and left it on the beach. I pretended that Dad was the enemy spy, and he'd caught me off guard and trapped me. That was fun for a while, until the sky got dark and it got cold; a summer storm. I couldn't believe it when my dad and my mom and Becky started to walk away, leaving me buried. Laughing, Dad helped me dig out, and as we ran back to the cabin, it began to pour, coloring the sugar-sand from the white kind to the brown. The next day there was a ten-foot hammerhead shark washed up on the beach. Stinky as it was, no one could stay away from it for long. *Jaws* wasn't a movie yet, or a book.

The biggest shell I have is a conch, rough like a shell on the outside, smooth pink on the inside. I hold it up to my ear now, like I used to. I can still hear Destin's blue-green waves inside, recorded forever, and I can close my eyes and almost feel the breeze and see the beach and the castles we used to build at the water's edge.

FIVE

The next morning I get to the Metronome a little early and grab a cheese Danish from the case in the café which shares space in the store. I stick a Styrofoam cup of coffee under the register, for when I go on.

I get a break near noon, and I walk around the store to stretch my legs and arms and neck. I look over the sound tracks, but there's nothing new except Quincy Jones' from *The Color Purple,* which is good, we've played a couple of sides on the stereo in the store; I think I must see the film before it leaves. Tears for Fears is nearly empty, like U2 and Phil Collins; Roberta Flack is full, and so is Streisand, which is always well stocked. In the back, I spot Bruce in the general area of Windham Hill, flipping through the George Winston. The last time I saw Bruce he was with Richard at Cooter's, a few weeks ago. They used to be lovers; Bruce got Richard hooked on coke and pot, then for a while had him as a slave—that's the way everybody who hears it, hears it. Richard once told me it was true, but he was wasted. Bruce smells funny back there, like some-one's done pot and poured brandy all over the place and hasn't washed in weeks, all together with the odd odor of burnt plastic. I know why he's here, looking for music to get high by, music to be inspired to decadence by. It revolts me to think about him, but I walk back there anyway to make sure the situation is jake.

"Hey, Deed, I hear you need some stuff, man," Bruce says. His blond hair is messed up, like if some mother scruffed it, saying how precious he was. There are circles under his dark eyes, and they're wide, his eyes, and they dart nervously from the displays to the racks to me, and back again. And something sticky and black has spilled on his jeans; one little tendril drips down his left leg.

"Who told you that?" I notice his zipper is down, too. Perhaps he's here fresh from a rape. From what Richard tells me, Bruce is one of the cops' regular pickups for the crimes they can't pin on anyone else. Personally, I think Bruce should be put away somewhere, to rot.

"Richard, yesterday. Said you were pretty shaken up." Bruce reaches over into the jazz section and pulls the first thing his hand lands on, an Al Jarreau. His other hand slips into his pocket.

"Maybe so. But I don't need anything," I say, very sure. If there's one thing I don't want to do today or any day, it's to get mixed up with this guy. I heard once that he cut someone's finger off over a five-dollar loan. Richard said he heard that Bruce even sliced some girl's nipple off—if I remember it right—just to see blood on her skin. It could have been that he cut her breast open. From what I hear about him, and from the way he always behaved in school, Bruce is something beyond dangerous. No one knows for sure if he's sick or not, but I'd be willing to guess, if anyone asked me, that he's several perversions *past* sick. I can't see how the guy survives. There must be more to him than what we all know, but I'll never find out what it is. If one thing's for sure, it's that the circle that used to hang with Bruce has died off—and I mean *died off,* one way or another—and that when Bruce says jump, you jump, when he says move, you move, like it or not.

"That's okay, no problem." His hand slips out of his pocket and I'm not really watching it until I hear the click, and suddenly he has a blade in his hand. For some strange, twisted reason, all I notice is that there's a coal mine of filth under his nails and all over his hand. He takes the blade and caresses the album-cover face of Al Jarreau. The point catches one of the track lights above, sparkling for a half second, and makes a soft, coughing hiss as it splits the cellophane. Another pass and the blade has cut a jagged circle around Al's head, then around quickly—like a virtuoso, Bruce does this—to decapitate the man completely. My eyes have been Super Glued there, and they follow the flipping head to the gray-carpet floor at Bruce's feet. It lands face down. I hear the click of the closing blade, and then Bruce bends down and picks up the face, snapping it like a Vegas dealer hits a blackjack hand of fourteen. Then, looking at me, Bruce hands me Al Jarreau's head.

Bruce doesn't say anything more, and there's nothing I want to say, so I walk away. I head for outside, the sun, but it isn't there, it's behind a huge cloud, and it's already begun to drizzle. "Shit," I say, but I stay out anyway, under the awning.

"Hey, dick, don't fuckin' mess with me, or I'll leave you cold in the gutter," I hear behind me. Bruce has come out whispering in force.

Hearing the voice without seeing the face throws me for a moment. It's not the *what,* but the *how.* I see suddenly the times—all lumped together, sort of—at Newman when Bruce used to threaten anyone smaller than himself. He did the usual pushing and shoving in lines, and hitting and pulling anything and anyone he could; several times I saw him fighting in the playground near school (he was smart enough not to fight on school grounds), always against three or four—and he always won. Once, back when I was in fourth grade and Bruce was in seventh, I remember seeing him cornering a girl and trying to tear her sweater. The principal happened to come along and pry Bruce's hands from the sweater (I saw the smudge later); he then tried to hold on to Bruce's arm. Bruce tore away from him and ran down the hall past me toward the library, where his idea was to shoot through the plate-glass swinging doors. But when his flying hand met the standing glass, his arm went right through. The bloodstains on the door remained as a warning; the scars up and down Bruce's arm remained as a testimony to his worthlessness.

Now, outside, he doesn't wait for a response, and I don't much feel like giving one. He just walks away, to the lot across the street, holding the record he didn't pay for in his sticky hand.

Later I end up at Cooter Brown's for a game and to straighten out Richard. I spot him in the back, taking another kid for quarters. But when I see him I decide not to tell him about Bruce, I can't figure out what good it would do. I go over instead to the dart boards and find that someone has left three red ones in a board. I throw badly for about fifteen minutes, then quit.

I leave and walk toward home. It's dark as I near the house where my first girl, Frankie, used to live. I was in tenth grade and just one wild night away from being a virgin; she was in ninth and not even close anymore. She had intriguing light brown eyes, dirty blond curls, the best kind of curvy body, and the most sparkling smile you ever saw, I ever saw. Anybody would have fallen the way I did, swept up in the breeze that always followed her. The breeze that eventually became a horrible stench.

I remember the way she squeezed into our lives,

through me, so quickly. Before any of us knew it, she had inspected the field and had already set into motion events which would destroy me, my father, and our lives. The mystery to me is how she knew the things she knew, the right buttons to push in us all; it was like she'd done some impossible research about us, before she met us, before she met me.

There are times I try to imagine what it was like for him, sneaking around with her. Where could they go? Did everyone in town know about it, and didn't anyone wonder who she was? Since then, I have discovered that the worst thing she did to me, maybe to us all, was to open the door to endless questions, questions which would never have occurred to me by themselves if I had not been burned—scorched, really—by her. It's the wondering, the questions, which make going back to how it was before so hard. It's the question of trust, of where the lines are drawn, of how I am to view someone who has betrayed me the way they did. The question which never goes away, no matter what.

All by itself, the trust question is one dipped in pain. Joined with the others, it takes on an importance I don't know how to describe. It colors everything. Everything.

Frankie used to warn me about her father, about how crazy he was, that if he thought we were sleeping together, he'd all but kill me. I guess it was me who should have worried about *my* father.

When Frankie was with me, it was like a dream. She was the girl I had been waiting for, a girl who was patient and loving, a girl who could and would teach me what I wanted to learn about everything from kissing to what we called "big s, big e, big x."

Sometimes I wonder what she could have known that my father wanted so much to learn.

I get closer to the house, and I can see someone standing in front, and it turns out to be Frankie herself, back from wherever she disappeared to. Someone told me she went to San Francisco, someone else said to Little Rock, where she was living with a black man. I heard her father disowned her, which didn't come as much of a surprise, considering.

I try to walk past, but don't make it. "Hi, Deed," I hear behind me. I stop, but don't turn around to look at her. "On your way home?"

"Yeah," I say, then turn to see her face in the moonlight. I see at once that it has not changed. Her hair is shorter than it was. If anything, her skin is smoother. She hasn't grown any taller (though I have) or lost any of her hazardous curve. She smiles, as if nothing extraordinary has happened between us before this moment. As if she had never met my father once. "I thought you moved away."

"I did, but I'm back now."

I see no point in talking to her. There were too many lies, too many fights, too much plain hurt in the end. I ask, "Why?" but it leaves a bitter taste in my mouth. I know standing here that I don't want to speak to her, that I'd be perfectly happy never to see her again. But I don't walk away. Maybe there's some stupid need to confront her now, to confront it all now. I think, NO, not now—

"Why do you sound so cold, Deed?" asks Frankie.

"I think you know."

"That was a long time ago, Deed. Haven't you forgotten it yet? Haven't you been able to go on?"

Her tone disgusts me, the way she seems to be speaking down to me, yet I stand there, still. The way she keeps saying my name bothers me, just like salesmen do, trying to get you to buy something you don't want. If there's one thing I hate, it's someone trying to sell me. Asshole salesmen. Frankie seems in their abysmal league.

"I've gone on. I thought about what you did for a few

days, not long, and I decided that it wasn't worth thinking about," I lie. "That *you* weren't worth thinking about." This is true. "I don't think about it, or you."

"Then why the cold shoulder? Hasn't anyone hurt you before?"

"Before and since. But I don't like being lied to."

"I never lied to you, Deed," Frankie says, the voice she used for sincere in perfect form. I remember it well.

"Look, I don't want to discuss it again. It's ridiculous to talk about it again. I don't have the time to waste—"

"Can't we just live with the past and be friends now? We shared—"

"No."

"Why not? Why is that so hard for you?"

"It's not hard," I say, swallowing. "It's not hard at all. But since then I have grown, and I've learned to trust. I know it used to be different, but now I choose my friends very carefully, I can afford that luxury. And I don't choose to have you as a friend. I don't have the time to waste on such a—" I stop myself, don't want to overdo it.

She doesn't say anything, she just looks at me in the darkness.

"Dad and Mom and them moved to San Francisco last year."

I stand there and remember how upset I was that I hadn't been able to meet her brother because he had died of pneumonia, long before I met her. Now I wish it was Frankie I had never met.

"I have to go." I walk away.

"Deed," she says, and sticks out her hand. Turned back around, I look at it, then at her face, and slowly shake my head no. After a moment, I walk away from her house. For a while I can feel her eyes watching me, for a block or so. Then the feeling is gone, and the walking is easier.

SIX

In all the years I knew him, he and I never really talked about it. It was just something that was there, how the guys never liked me, like they did him. Sure, it was important to me, but it didn't have any connection to our growing friendship. And to tell the truth, I was a little afraid to bring it up; if I'd forced Jason to choose, maybe he'd have chosen them.

The first thing he and I had in common was the swings. We discovered this connection in sixth grade. For years, he was the first one at the swings in Green Trees, at Newman, a small park filled with the shade of huge trees, maybe oaks. There, the guys played sports, the girls just played, and Jason swung.

He used to swing back and forth, gaining speed and momentum with each pass, until he was just a blond-haired blur in the dusty, sun-streaked shade. His eyes were closed. I used to wonder what he was thinking about as he flew through the air. Higher and higher he'd go, until he was as high as the horizontal bar the swing was chained to, until a teacher ripped him out of his flying trance with a shrill voice.

More than his swinging, it was the way he got off the swings that really took hold of the class' attention. He had two ways, either to drop his feet and drag them on the dirt, raising a brown cloud, or just jumping off, in the middle of a powerful upward swing. Those times, Jase'd spread his arms and legs out wide, as if to actually take off, then land like a cat about ten yards away, in a grassy patch.

It was something to see.

Even his pals, the guys, were awed by his recklessness.

I had fun in Green Trees, too, in my own way. I used to carve out sections of bark from the trees until I reached the light-colored core. There, from between the wood fibers, came sap, every spring, without fail. One year I carved a path in the bark from the core to the ground, and rigged a plastic cup to catch the drooling sap. By the week's end, the cup was filled, and though the result was a series of science classes devoted to plants and syrup, I was a hero for a while. It was the only time.

The next fall, the start of seventh grade, I saw the result of the holes in the trees. I was forbidden to carve into the trees again, the teachers told me, because I'd left them open to the winter, and death.

Which left me Jason's swings. That was okay, since there were three (one, the fourth, had a torn seat), the best being the one on the end, the one Jason always used. Naturally, that was the one I wanted. Every day at eleven-fifteen, I had to race him to it, winner take all. He was sure fast, but so was I on a good day. Though I never beat him there, I came close a couple of times, which showed him I wasn't as worthless as he'd thought.

Eventually, we became friendly, and not long after that, he defied his pals by speaking to me during gym like I was a real friend. Gym class was the real testing ground. Before a boy became a boy, he had to be one of the guys at gym.

Later that same year, in the spring, we started playing softball. On one day that season, I was up to bat in the last few minutes of class, with the bases loaded and my team one run down. The captain of my team, Marty, asked the coach if I could be replaced at the last minute because he didn't believe I could do it. The coach, who had only weeks before taken me out of a football game so that I could fold sweaty varsity jerseys, somehow saw that Marty was wrong, and so I stood there, bat in the air, staring at the pitcher. Jason was primed on second, ready to sprint, and looking at me. He and I both knew that if I could just hit the ball, I could certainly run to the base. A good hit would win us the game.

Pitches streaked by, and before I knew it, I had two strikes, three balls, and most of the class against me. The next pitch was the end of the game, and the end of me, if I screwed up. Standing there, I wondered what would make them happier, my hitting the ball well or fucking up again and proving them all right about me—again.

I knew I had to swing. Jason's eyes, behind the pitcher, were on me.

"Time out!" I said. I walked around a little, kicked the dust, then took my stance again. I put a look on my face that I wished would tell everyone that I was determined to hit the ball out of town.

The pitcher shot the ball wide, but I stepped into it and swung, my eyes closed. The crack it made sounded like a gun, and not knowing where the ball was or how far it had gone, I dropped the bat and ran for first, pretending all I wanted was to get to that swing in Green Trees before Jason. A few seconds later, the bell sounded and class was over.

Directly across from me, at home plate, the team had Jason in the air. We'd won. It was my hit that had sent Jason across the plate to win the game, yet Jason was in the air. And I was alone on second, surrounded by dust and sunlight.

All I could do was watch. I didn't even hear the cheers. I just saw Jason bouncing on their arms. Then he spotted me.

In a kind of silly slow motion, they put him down. Still they crowded around him, patting him on the back, on his ass, messing up his hair. He had a clear view of me, though, and we stared at each other. We both knew he was in a place I would never be.

At that moment, though, for the first time, his place was the only place I *wanted* to be. For once, I wanted to have that.

His eyes were on me. I could see he was trying to brush them all away, like he was suddenly embarrassed by it all. But they wouldn't move. After all, he'd won their game for them. Finally, he surrendered to it, to them, and just before he turned away from me, to his friends, he shrugged, leaving me to understand.

It's my day off. I go to a bookstore to find some poems by Sylvia Plath, but they're out of the book I want. I don't go to another store; by now, the urgent need to read her is gone. It's like being terribly horny on a night there's no one to screw, and going to the stand to get a new skin book because the ones you have are too old and you know all the pictures and letters by heart now, but when you get there, there just isn't anything that you really want to spend the ten bucks on. And you don't go to another stand because by then the hard-on is gone and you've lost your appetite for it.

What I buy is *Goldfinger,* the James Bond book. Before she was killed, my mother gave all her Bond paperbacks to the Symphony Book Fair or something. It occurs to me now that the man's name, Goldfinger, is too sexual to pass up, though I know this observation is too obvious not to have been written about in magazines for years. I leaf through, trying to remember the flick. It's foggy, though. All I can remember is a chick called Pussy Galore, which is hard to forget, and I figure that's a good enough reason to get it.

I walk the two blocks to the Grill. I don't see Michael anywhere, so I walk straight to the office in the back, past the counter and through a swinging door into the kitchen, past the bathrooms and past a black woman kneading pie-crust dough, past a black man scrubbing a huge sink of pots and pans and another black man making beef patties. Then up a small staircase and through a door with steel bars across the foot-by-foot window, where I find Michael, like always, with the manager. The manager has been here for years, used to be the doorman. I tell him hey, and I realize I don't know his name. But I don't ask, either. Michael says, "Hey, man," and he's smoking. I never knew he smoked. "How you doin'?"

Michael calls everyone "man," even Becky, when we're here for dinner when she's in town. Becky, a year older than I am, is in college in Pennsylvania, studying something or other, I'm not sure. Whenever she's in town we spend a lot of time at the Grill's counter, talking. Though I was a rotten brother when we were kids, we've grown closer recently, since she left town "for the end of the rainbow," as she says. I have the feeling she'll find it, and soon. She's that kind of girl. Last time we spoke, she said there was even a guy, Jeff. She said she thought maybe they were the ends of each other's rainbows.

"Good," I say to Michael, "how are you?"

"Can't say much, man. You in for lunch?"

"Yeah," I say, and Michael nods his approval. Some days he tells them I can have it on the house, but today no such luck, but I have the money, I got paid yesterday.

"What you reading, man?"
"*Goldfinger,* the Bond book," I say.
"Cool enough, man."
"You read it?"
"Saw the movie."
"Yeah. I hope the book's as good," I say. "How's your mom?" Then the phone rings. I stand there as he answers, thinking about how thin she was the last time I saw her. I look at Michael and he motions for me to go eat, that he'll be out there in a while.

I walk back through the kitchen, out to the dining room, and there's a seat right on the end. Harry doesn't work days, so Benny's on today. I tell him I don't need a menu, I'm ready.

He says okay.

I order, and Benny takes his red pencil and makes marks on the menu slip next to what I want. Then he slides the slip under the salt shaker, facing it in so he can read it as he walks by, later.

I watch the chef turn my burger for the second time, and press down on it with his spatula, and the grease squirts from it and sizzles on the hot grill. I spot Chip on the other side, in the opposite end seat. His head wobbles on his neck, and he looks sick.

I get up and walk over to him.

"Chip?"

He doesn't hear me, but I don't say it again because I know it won't do any good. There's a seat next to him, and I sit down, my hand on his shoulder. He feels hot, like burning. His face is sweaty, his skin whiter than usual, clammy and chalky. Chip turns his face in my direction, looks at me, but his eyes don't register. They're on me, but look through me, sort of; past me. There are red blotches, stains, on his hands, between his fingers.

I can't eat now, and moving Chip isn't even a question

—it just wouldn't do any good. I know that. He looks worse than ever before.

When I leave, I push open the first of the two doors, and I'm still fixed on Chip, so I don't even see Dottie walking in.

As I make it through the door, she elbows me hard enough to make me look at her. I see her black eyes behind the white Ray-Bans. She stares at me, recognizes me from one meeting months ago, then moves inside. I know Bruce did that to her, and she knows I know it. Maybe he got her pregnant again and she won't get rid of it this time. It's happened twice before. The first time, she had an abortion, which he didn't pay for; the second time, she didn't know she was pregnant until one day she went to the bathroom and miscarried into the toilet by accident. As Dottie shoves past, I smell Bruce in the air, and a shiver sprints the length of my spine.

As I walk along Carrollton, I begin to think about Marian, and I decide to walk up to her place and apologize for leaving so abruptly the other night. For the first time, I feel . . . guilt? Maybe. It's probably because we fucked, and I knew what she wanted me to say, and I didn't say it, or couldn't, but I was horny and fucked her anyway. Dammit.

When I get there, there's no answer, she must be at work or something; I didn't even think of looking in Häagen-Dazs first. So I get on a streetcar and head for home.

The streetcar rolls its way back toward St. Charles, past the Grill. In front of the Grill are two police cars and an ambulance. Michael has come out of his office, to the street. As the streetcar floats by, I see Chip on a stretcher, two men in white wheeling him out. The streetcar stops at the next stop, half a block away, and I think, Should I get off and go over there? What am I supposed to *do?*

Without an answer of any kind, I stand up and walk to the back door of the streetcar, the exit door. It doesn't open automatically; you have to push against the hydraulics that keep it closed. When I push on the one with the vertical bar, the thing won't budge. I can't muster the strength I need to pry open the door. I see through the glass that they're loading Chip away. Finally, the door is open enough for me to squeeze through. But I don't move. I just stand there. "Hey, you gettin' off, man?" I hear from the front, from the driver, but still I remain cemented there. Suddenly, in a split second, I know that it will be impossible for me to get off the streetcar. Going over there to see him, dead, would drop me right in the middle of everything I don't want to be in the middle of. Chip's had this other life ever since I met him, and I chose not to know about it, not to ask him about it, not to be involved in it at all. It was like he had this secret underground life, totally separate from mine, and the one we shared. I don't even know what there was in his other world. I never wanted to know. Something clues me in, though, right now, about what it was. Maybe it's that Dottie was in there with him, just now. Maybe not. I don't know for sure. It probably doesn't matter. What matters most is that I am not going to step foot out of this streetcar. I am not going over to the Grill to find out what happened to my friend.

When the streetcar starts moving, after I have taken my seat again, I don't even look back to see, I just sit there and try to get Chip's chalky, chiseled, OD'd face out of my eyes. When I finally look back, as the streetcar makes the turn onto St. Charles, the ambulance is gone, no sirens, no lights. (I suddenly remember one day walking with Chip downtown, a couple of years ago, and we saw a woman on a bike get hit by a car. Someone called an ambulance, and it arrived maybe fifteen minutes later, sirens and lights all the way. We heard them for blocks in the noonday traffic. They loaded the woman into the back, and a couple of minutes later they drove away, no sirens, no lights . . .) One of the policemen is walking Dottie out, but he doesn't put her into a car, he just lets her walk away.

One of the policemen I recognize from the other night, at Jason's. This hasn't been his week. Come to think of it, it hasn't been *my* week. What's . . . ?

I sit there, eyes propped open by the shock of it, and by the cool wind. I try, I try to find something to think about, something to distract me from this, from Chip's face, and from Jason's. It's like, will there ever be anything powerful enough to make my eyes tear themselves away from these damned ghost images? As a distraction, even the wonderment is a failure. It all hangs there . . . waiting for me to reach it, to pass it, but I never get any closer.

I turn around, and I notice an old woman at the back of the streetcar, asleep, a stuffed shopping bag at her feet. Her cane is on the floor beneath her, jerking with the motion of the streetcar. There's a fly on her leg, sniffing the varicose veins, stubborn against the wind rushing through.

SEVEN

The bathroom is so white, absolute, like a temple, a porcelain tomb. The color of the jackets on the men who took Jason away, the color of Chip's skin at the Grill, the color of the rim of Dottie's Ray-Bans.

I think, There are so many ways to do it in this room. Pills, bottles of pills. Drowning, in the tub or the toilet. Or the mirror glass, after you wrapped the towel around your hand and shattered it and used one of the shards to . . .. Or the razor blades would be easier, the old kind, the ones my dad used to put in his steel razor, the one that's all rusty now.

"One day you'll be doing this, Walt." He stood there and looked like a skinny Santa, with a close beard, shaving it off.

"Does it hurt?" I asked, looking up at him.

"No, it . . . tickles."

"What's that?" I asked, pointing to the can with the red and white stripes.

"Shaving cream. Here, look," he said, bending down, and I smelled the menthol on his face, and he squirted some of the white foam on my hand. I jumped when it came out and made that noise.

"Put that on your cheek."

It felt cold there, and I said, "Cold, Daddy."

"Mm-hmm," he mm-hmmed, and stood up again. "One day soon, Walt, you'll do this. And one day you'll tell your boy about it, just like this."

I turned around and looked at my foamy face in the full-length on the back of the bathroom door . . .

The same door. Maybe even the same blades. I don't know, it doesn't matter.

My figure in the mirror is taller. About five foot ten, stringy brown hair, which used to be as sunny as my mom's. Rounded features which perfectly cross my mother's parents' with my father's parents'. Except for the almond eyes, a new shape, maybe to see new things. Or old things new ways. I wonder if Dad'll remember that day when he gets home from work and sees me here. I wonder, but not for long.

I catch my face in the mirror over the sink and see a little boy with his mother at the zoo, tossing the crusts to the ducks, and the boy doesn't know his mother will be dead very soon, too soon, and my dad with the boy, trying to enjoy throwing a spiral or making a basket from across the backyard, and the boy called "out," never "safe," in gym and crying until it was over and praying that the month at camp would end so he could go home and it would be over, all be over, and my father crying, and I am crying in the mirror, and I see the tears lost in the sink, first clear, then red.

Red tears, so many of them, a stream, nearly, on the floor, too, then . . .

I feel the cold white on my cheek.

EIGHT

I open my eyes and I'm in a white room, but not the bathroom. I'm in a bed, a goddamn white bed, and I catch someone leaving the room, and the door takes a few seconds to slowly swing shut. Outside in the hall I catch a woman with the sun on her face. I think, That's impossible, because no one can be that beautiful, that old, and then I remember that this is It, and then I realize that her white smock isn't a white smock at all, but wings. I try to keep hold of the face of the woman.

I think I see my dad standing over me. I think my eyes are open because I think I see him, and I think he's talking to me, saying, "Son . . . Deed . . . Can you hear me?" and I think, Yeah, but I don't say anything because . . . And he goes on, saying, I think, "Can you hear me? . . . We, we love you, Deed, we love you . . ." and he begins to cry for the second time in my life.

It happens again, only this time he isn't alone, Becky and my mom are with him, and I close my eyes for a moment and then open them again and it's just my dad and my sister, home from school, and I can't believe it because I'm— "We love you."

"I love you, too," I say, and they both cry. Later they tell me I hadn't cut far enough in, I'd fucked it up.

Marian appears one day, smiling as if nothing was ever wrong. She has been crying. She sits on the edge of my bed. "Hi," she says, her voice shaky.

"Hi," I say. I smile the best I can and look away from her face. In her hand there's a grease-stained bag from Mrs. Fields'.

"These are for you," I hear her say, then look back up, and she is crying again. She hands me the bag, then runs her sleeve across her face, smearing the tears. I open it; inside are six oatmeal-raisins. I eat one even though I'm not too hungry now. It's still warm and buttery, perfect. "Are you okay?"

"Yeah, fine, nothing serious. They're letting me go home tomorrow."

"Good," she says, and for a second I wonder what that means. She takes my hand and holds it; hers is hot, clammy.

This is not the Marian I met at Häagen-Dazs, not by a long shot. The girl I met at Häagen-Dazs was strong, she knew exactly what she wanted, and she wasn't going to take any bullshit, or anything less. But this girl is a far cry from that. This girl is so terribly, so obviously weak, and it's so . . . unattractive. I mean, if she wants a commitment, this isn't the way to get it. I don't respond well to guilt, and I could never love someone I only pity. Could it really be just my hesitancy that's caused this change in her? I hope it isn't, yet I know that it is, at once.

Even her hair, the Alabama-red waves she used to toss back with a flick of her chin, even that's different; now her hair seems flat, stringy, gross. Something is missing from this Marian, something more than this thing we have, or don't have, and I know pretty much for sure that I don't care what it is. And that's pretty terrible, after all that's brought us here.

I want to tell her I'm sorry for the other night, but I don't know how long ago that was. I want to tell her about Chip, and Dottie, and walking over there the other day, but I don't know how long ago that was, either. All I can think of, even now, is her leaving. It suddenly becomes painfully obvious that I don't want to see her again, that I don't want to feel this way ever again, like I've done something very wrong. I wish I could do it, just wrap the package in a tidy ribbon, tie up all the loose ends. But maybe it's better just to let it—and her—fade away.

Richard opens the door around seven. He pokes his head in to see if I'm asleep, but I'm not. I tell him to come in and sit. He's got his INXS T-shirt on, and I wouldn't notice it, but on Richard it seems to say more.

"They told me what happened," he says.

"Oh, yeah?" I say.

"I never thought you'd . . ."

"Neither did I, I guess."

"Bruce said he saw you at work and you seemed upset."

"Did he? When did you see him?"

"Yesterday. In jail."

I don't say anything now, I just wait for it.

Richard looks out the window. "He almost killed Dottie," and I close my eyes, hung on the word "almost" and groping for a way to shut him off, or out, but Richard's voice keeps coming. "She was pregnant again. He beat her. The baby's gone. He won't be out for a long time. They found some crack in his place, and some coke, and she was full of it herself. When they found 'em there, she was on the floor, undressed. He'd tried to shoot her up, after she was out. One of the needles had snapped off. I went down to see him. He said it was an accident. His face was all red, crying. He was a mess. I don't think he meant to hu—"

"Stop it," I say then. At that moment, a question occurs to me, but I don't ask it, not out loud anyway.

Why?

It's a question that rings in my head, trapped somewhere between my ears, in that perpetually revolving door that admits and expels every thought, every sound.

Now, *why* occurs to me as *the* question. An answer to it, a good answer, should be the end. *The* answer. But it won't come, I know it won't, not from Bruce and Dottie, not from Richard, not from me—not now. Probably because it isn't as important as moving forward, past all this.

"Stop it. Please, just stop it now. I don't want to hear about Bruce or Dottie again," I say quietly. "Please."

"Okay . . . I understand. I brought you something," he says, and takes something out of his pocket. An eight ball, from Cooter Brown's. He puts it in my hand. It feels heavy and cold; I like the feel of it. I look at him.

"Thanks, thanks a lot."

"Use it in good health," he says, and laughs a little. After a moment, I laugh, too, a little, for the first time in . . .

A while later, Richard stands up to leave. At the door he says, "I'm off the stuff, Deed. No shit this time." I look at his face hard, in the shadow, because I want to believe he means it this time, but I don't see it. I don't believe him. INXS. He leaves, and the door slowly swings shut behind him.

I get up and walk over to the window. It's already open a crack, so I open it the rest of the way. I look out into the cool night. Buildings, just buildings. A horn, a screech.

I wait for the sound of the collision.

It doesn't come.

I lean on the sill, and the cold steel burns my arm

through the pj fabric. But I keep my arm there. It burns, but it's nice. I like feeling it. Feeling something. I pull back the sleeve and lay my bare arm back on the steel, and quick, like a match lighting, there's a burning line from my elbow to where the bandage is wrapped around my wrist.

The feeling seems incomplete, so I remove the gauze. The stitches are still there, and my skin is chalky, drained. Red, white, and the blue thread. I touch it, I run my finger over it, the place, the wound. The skin there is smooth, only dappled a little from the gauze. I press my palm against the wound, and it's . . . not warm. Well, maybe warm. Maybe . . .

—Alive.

So I turn it over and press the wound onto the steel, and the cold burns there, but I don't take it off. I press harder, looking first out at the buildings, then back at my arm. It stings, and all I want to do is move it . . .

Then it goes away. The burning dies slowly. Dies until having the wound on the steel is no big thing.

I turn it over again and look at it. Now the skin has some color. Blue. Murky, but blue.

The eight ball is on the bed. I grab it, cold and heavy in my hand. I hold it tightly and pump my fingers against it. The veins under the blue inflate madly, like a garden hose, and the blue turns red.

Another screech. I wait for it.

Nothing.

I wind up and hum the eight ball out over the rooftops. Its smooth surface catches the streetlights and the security lights, so I can see it all the way down. Then it disappears into the shadows. I wait for it . . .

—and it hits.

Its death echoes among the walls right back to me. Perfect.

Sleep's a cinch then.

NINE

I see the woman when they wheel me out of my room, on the way out. A nurse is behind me, my dad on the side, and Becky.

She's in the hall outside my room, like she's waiting for me. Her face is lined and fallen, sort of, and what used to be there is obvious; there's a kind of beauty, a brightness. It's in her eyes, the way they're alive. Her hair is so white, so . . . angelic, so safe. I keep my eyes on her face even though she doesn't see me, and before we turn the corner and I lose her, I jump out of the chair and run back to her. I catch her and stop, out of breath.

She turns to me and says, "Hello, there," and smiles.

"Hi," I say, panting, and then I don't know what to say, so I just look at her face and smile.

"My name is Kate," she says, and the smile never leaves her face. Suddenly I am nervous without knowing why; I feel like I'm on trial or something. "Do you have time to talk?" she says. I look back at my dad, who is looking at me, puzzled. I turn back to Kate.

"Come on," she says, taking my hand. She leads me into a small room with plastic chairs.

"No, don't stop," I say.

"What?"

"Smiling."

"Why?" she says, and smiles.

"Because I like it when you smile. When I first saw you, you were smiling. I thought I saw . . ." and I realize that this is going to sound stupid.

"What did you see?"

"I thought I saw the sun on your face."

"Really?"

Now I smile, very embarrassed, and say, "Yeah. I saw it only a second, outside my room, through the door."

She doesn't say anything. She just looks at me, and her eyes dart over my face. I wonder what she could be thinking; is it about me?

She looks away for a moment then, down at the floor, then for just a moment somewhere higher, somewhere on me. My bandages. My *wrist.* Her eyes remain there for a moment too long; she's seen it, added it up. Then she looks back at me, that smile.

"Can I ask you a question? Why were you here that day?"

"Just for some tests," she says. "I have them once a year."

"Oh," I say, and my dad opens the door to the room, then walks in with Becky and a doctor and the nurse.

"Ready to go, Deed?"

I look at them all, waiting for me, and I say, "Yeah, sure." I stand up, and the nurse holds the wheelchair for me. My father walks over to Kate and introduces himself.

"Do you know Deed?"

"I do now," she says, and then looks at me and winks.

"Would you like to have some lunch with us, Kate?" my Dad asks, then turns to look at me. I smile at him, surprised, and I see instantly that he knows I am shocked—

and is pleased that I am. Oddly, though, this time his pleasure, I'm sure, is not malicious. Oddly.

"I'd love to," Kate says.

After lunch, Kate and I sit in my room at home. We talk a little; for some reason I trust her from the start, like I trust my grandmother, I feel like I could tell her everything, caught up in her warmth.

"Why, Deed?"

"Why." I look around my room, at the things on the walls, the movie posters, a picture of my mother (her engagement picture, in black and white). A gondolier's hat with the red ribbon, stuffed animals, my bulletin board with all the pins stuck into it: "Think Japane$e," "I'm wickedly delicious," "Vote Kennedy," "E.T. Lives." And Mardi Gras beads.

"I was always the kid everybody laughed at. I never played sports very well, and at Newman, sports was the thing you had to do best, or else. Once, in a gym class, I managed to hit the ball into center field, and I ran around the bases, and between second and third the ball was thrown to the catcher or someone, who threw it to third. And everyone said to keep running, so I ran as fast as I could, and when I got there, they said I was out, and all the guys were laughing at me, teasing me. All except the guys on my team, who were yelling at me, which was much worse, 'cause it was like I let them down. What it was, was that I didn't know. So during school no one liked me very much because I didn't know the rules to any of their games. I really didn't care about them, either. I remember when I was seven, just before my mother died, she told me to go to school and play, to pretend I wanted to, because then the boys would see that at least I was interested, and they would like me for trying. But I told her no, and I thought, I want them to like me for me, not because I play some stupid game. But they never even wanted to know about me. They didn't care who I was, just because I didn't know how to play. They only cared how fast I could run, or how many touchdowns I could make. People are only interested in what they know, what's familiar. Anything else is suspect. People don't even want to know about anything new because it might wreck what they already have, or what they think about, or how they think about things. People never notice that they're not really living. They're just existing. They do what's expected of them—I mean most everyone I know and see around—they do what's expected or they don't do it, but either way, they don't care about it. They don't take an interest in what they're doing, even. They don't take a stand, or have an opinion. It's just *do* or *not do,* you know? And doing it or not doesn't really matter to them, because they don't really care about their lives. They don't try anything new. They never want to accomplish anything. They're satisfied to be average. They don't try to be the best they can be, and they don't even *think* like that. It's like they're afraid to. Like if they try, they might fail, and failing would be worse in their eyes than going for it. They'd say it's better not to try because failing's a terrible thing, it's better to sit around just like everybody else, doing what everybody else does. They don't see that it doesn't matter if you fail as long as you learn from it, as long as you tried. To me . . . to me, suicide isn't what I tried to do. It's not the end of life, but . . . the absence of it."

I look around the room, wondering what it was that started *that.* The sun's pouring in through the windows.

"You see? I see these people and all I want to do is scream. All I want to do is stop everything for a while, to catch my breath. When I was in that bathroom"—I point to it—"I felt totally alone, and I was perfectly happy to *be* alone, yet . . . all I wanted was someone to be there to stop me."

I stand up and walk around the room. "Is it wrong to want what I want? Is it a mistake to want . . . more? Is it dumb to think like this, to think about things like this, that it's okay for me to be alone, yet still want to be surrounded by friends? Is it wrong, mostly, to hold on to all the memories, and to let them be a big part of the way I live now?" I look over at her, on a wooden chair with a cushion, the only one in the room. Her smile is gone, her eyes red.

I walk over to the bulletin board and there's a picture of my mother. I am in her arms, and she is smiling down at me. "Ever since I was a little boy," I begin to say, caught up in the momentum of the memory, "I wondered what it would be like to be hit by a truck."

There, it's been said out loud for the first time, admitted, like some dark secret, some silly, sick thing that's been tucked away for . . . ever, as long as I can remember. The picture brought it all back, too real, too much. Stark pictures everywhere, my mother, all of us, when I was a boy. All before. Enough emotion to fill . . . yet I am the only one here now. And I am filled, filled so that it needs to pour out of me, and now. Kate is here, but no longer here.

I continue. "My mother was a teacher, an English teacher, and I remember one day when I was little she brought home a stack of pictures from school. Pictures of people who had been beaten up, people who had been burned. I had never seen those things before, and I didn't like seeing them. I don't even know why she had them, or brought them home. But I couldn't stop thinking about them, those people, what had put them into those situations. I wanted to know what it felt like to be in their shoes. I don't mean I thought about it like that, but the feeling was there, the words to describe it came later. You know, like telling Mom no when she said to go and play football. I didn't know the words about why, but I knew why. It was the same with the feeling about the pictures. What did it feel like to be on fire? What did it feel like to be hit by someone, really hit, slapped across the face so hard you bled? My mother died soon after that. She was killed in an accident. The school sent all her stuff home, her private files. My dad put it all in the attic, with all her clothes, after the funeral. They stayed up there for years and years, until last winter. It was Christmas Day, and I missed her so much that day, and I went up there to find a sweater of hers. I wanted to smell her. I know that sounds silly, but I wanted to feel that she was there. I found the sweater I was looking for. It was in an old trunk with all her other stuff. I had that sweater in my hands and I buried my face in it in the dark, all alone. But there wasn't anything there. There was no smell at all. It just smelled like the attic, all musty and . . . dead. It smelled empty, that's what I mean, empty. When I found it and I couldn't smell her, I knew she was dead for real, that I couldn't bring her back. I sat in that attic and smelled everything there was, old skirts and rags, even an old perfume bottle, but it was all dried out inside. And then at the bottom of the trunk were those pictures, all yellowed and worn. Somehow that made them worse than I remembered. I took them to my room and hid them between the mattresses. I used to look at them late at night, when Dad and Becky were asleep. There was a woman who was beaten by her husband, I guess; her face was bloody and cut, and her eyes had black-black circles under them, and she was crying when they took the picture. All those old feelings came back. I wanted to know why he had done this to her, and now I knew enough to be able to find the words I needed. That was the difference, being able to think about it, and not just feel it. That year I was in a writing class. The teacher said that writers write what they know, and the more they know, the better they write. I thought that was wrong. I thought if you could really write, then you could make up anything you needed to know. I tried to write a story about that woman in the picture, and about some other people faced with the same kinds of things, death in certain situations . . . but I couldn't do it. I didn't know how it felt to be beaten like that, to be on the edge. I couldn't make that up. Pretty soon I began to think about the truck again, getting hit by it. I wanted to know how it would feel at the moment you were hit by it and sent flying out in front of it. All the time I spent thinking about it, I couldn't make it real to myself. I wanted the people who read it to feel the truth, but it was impossible for me. I couldn't write it because I . . . because I didn't know the truth. I didn't know it. So, when you ask me why I tried to commit suicide, I have to say I didn't, not really. I didn't want to kill myself, not like Chip, maybe, and Jason. Maybe. I think they wanted to die, or at least they really thought about it, enough so that they did. I didn't want to die. I just wanted to be alone. I wanted it all to be over for a while, that's all. I only wanted to really feel something, something . . . complete. I wanted to feel what it was like to be on the edge of death, but not to die. I wanted to come back . . . I wanted to come back."

I stop talking and I'm on the floor in front of Kate, and she has bent down, her arms around me, and she whispers, "You did." I look up at her and she's been crying, and I haven't even noticed her this whole time, and I begin to cry, too, and put my head back down. More than anything I want to get the pictures out of my mind, to free them from where they're kept, to free me from where I'm kept, the pictures of that battered woman and her black-black eyes, and of Chip at the Grill, his coffee-and-cream skin gone white, and Jason on the floor of that bathroom, the blood and the water running together in the shower, caught in the drain spiral, and his eyes, his wide eyes, frightened and panicked and resisting.

Alone in my room with everything I have ever accumulated, I hold the picture of my mother, the one where she has me in her arms and she is smiling down at me. For the first time, I think about what was going on in her mind when the shot was taken. Maybe she was thinking about what I would become, and how it would be determined by what I'd come from.

In the picture, her long, dark hair is pulled up and twisted. Her nails are kind of long, with red polish on them. Her eyes are squinted above her wrinkled nose, in her smile.

I go up to the attic, where my dad keeps everything he has ever accumulated, to find the old box, the one the oldest photos are kept in. I remember seeing it before, sometime, a reddish-brown box, not too large, rectangular.

In a corner, under a pile of old clothes, I find the box. Its lid is inlaid with other pieces of wood, and the design is of a blacksmith hammering a piece of iron on an anvil, if that's what it's called. The whole thing looks royal, the detail is all there, mostly in the shading of the smith's face; the box maker used different-colored woods to get it just right.

When I lift the lid, it swings back on hinges until two leather strips across the corners hold it high in place. The box is filled with black-and-whites, mostly, but there are others. The one on top is of me, an old school picture, from when I was at Newman. Two teeth are absent from my smile, which looks as happy as any seven-year-old's can be, I guess. My hair is wet and straight, specially prepared for this shot. From the wetness, you can't tell it's still blond, before the change, which came later. My mother never saw that.

There are many pictures of my mother in here. All her different hairstyles—when it was long, down her back; when it was all one length, down around her ears, when, I remember, she used to lace her fingers through it to get it back out of her eyes; when it was ponytailed all the time when she took a sculpting class, when she did the models of Becky's face and my face, now downstairs in the living room. And there's one of her next to the big piece she did which my grandmother has at her house.

The wedding pictures. She was so thin then, and so young, like my father. How fancy they were, all dressed up like that! My dad in tails, my mom in a long white gown, with millions of tiny pearls sewn into the lace. And them dancing. How old would my mother be now? Forty, maybe.

Becky with her reddish hair all frizzy, her face colored with Mom's makeup, and Mom's hands putting even more on. The baby pictures of Becky are a little further down, pictures of Becky in a small tub, all shiny and wet, and Becky on her stomach, her legs up, her face laughing at the camera.

Some of me and my dad in the backyard, playing catch, an old, stiff glove on my left hand. My dad's arm around me, and in his other hand, a bat, its tip in the grass. There's a shadow falling on us in the shot, the shadow of the photographer, probably Mom.

This picture, like all the others, I take from the box and stack on the floor, face up. When I look back into the box, now half empty, I see a page of newspaper, folded many times over. It's browner than the fresh copies of the *Times-Picayune* which are thrown into the driveway every morning. I carefully take the piece of paper out of the wooden box, then gently unfold it. Flattened on the hardwood floor of the attic, lit by flashlight, the page from the *Picayune* is from the obituaries. An article on the bridge accident that killed my mother. *News.*

My hands tremble some, and I put them together, each holding on to the other. Their trembling stops, then I have no one to hold on to me. Halfway through it, I stop to weep.

A long time after, I fold it back up again and put it in the pile of pictures. I know I must finish the box, I must climb this twisted tree of memories.

Below where the paper had been are many, many pictures of my parents' parents. Suddenly, I become amazed at the stories which pour out of the box. One photo is of all four grandparents, young and smiling, in Europe somewhere, with dozens of pigeons pecking and swooping all around. They must have known each other before the son met the daughter, or maybe they were childhood friends—either way, something I never knew.

And there's a series of pictures of my mother's mother —now the grandmother I don't see—when she was some sort of model back in the twenties. She has on in one picture a tight skirt with tassels all over it, and in another, a close-up, a hat that tightly covers her head, and the tassels on it match the ones on the skirt.

At the very bottom of the box are pictures taken during the birthday parties for Becky and me when we were young. Becky's birthday is a week before mine, on May 11, so the parties we had were for us both, with all her school friends and all the boys from school who were never to become mine. One year a pony ride in the yard, another year a carousel party at the park, another year a swimming party at my grandmother's house. The parties continued until I was ten, I think, and when Becky was eleven, which was when our dad lost interest in big events. From then on, birthdays were private.

Slowly and very carefully, I put the pictures back into the reddish box, over the folded page from the *Picayune,* which I lay securely on the bottom.

History. It fills the wooden box, it fills my head, there in the flashlighted attic space. I feel the weight of it all, yet the terrible absence of much more. Finally, I have a definite sense of what could have been, yet wasn't, for me, but really for all of us. In this box, my own history has been frozen in times photographed; where I come from is now kept here in this box. Where I go, past what is, beyond what might have been, the future—that is up to me. Sitting on the dusty floor, the box before me closed tight, its history safe, I promise myself to make up for what might have been, somehow. The keys to it, I think, are truth, which I had before and which I want again, and love, the kind I have never had, but desperately need.

Eyes closed, I see the last image, of me, a baby in my mother's arms, and she is smiling down at me, surely thinking about what I will become.

TEN

In the middle of the night I wake up, lost. Familiar things slowly appear in the lightening darkness. Finally I know where I am. Hearing only the ticks of my clock, I tiptoe across to my desk. At the back of the middle drawer is the folder I keep my papers in: old letters, pictures of all of us when I was a boy, when Mom was alive, my favorite picture of myself (an old black-and-white, me on the front steps of the house, one leg crossed horizontally over the other, my chin in a hand; I look so serene, yet inside, I know that everything's screwed up, with Mom gone, and with school; it's the subtext only I know about that makes the picture for me), and the paragraphs.

Twelfth grade, Mrs. Simmons' assignment one week was to write single-effect paragraphs. One paragraph to convey one idea, one emotion, one thought (and here's the kick), without actually stating it.

There are two in the folder now, maybe there were never more than two, I can't remember; one with a red-ink comment from her. For Christmas, some of us had gotten together to buy her a paperback romance called *Fleur,* which was her first name. She laughed.

The pictures of those people. The truck. The need to feel. I read the paragraphs over, and the only word that comes to mind is "desperate." Even then.

> As the metal cone streaked through space, its occupants began to feel the searing heat of reentry. The astronauts knew they were safe, protected by the silvery shield behind them. On the outside, the steely surface began to crack, leaving gaping holes—

This is where Mrs. Simmons, Fleur, has written "trite?" in red. I open the drawer and take out a short yellow pencil, dull. I make a line through "gaping holes" and write in the margin: "jagged craters."

> —leaving jagged craters where the covering once had been. As its speed increased, the tiny ship entered the seemingly rocky atmosphere of the planet. The astronauts felt huge boulders ram the ship, breaking and tearing into its layer of armadillo skin. The heat shield turned to a sunny orange, then to a cloudy white. Down its center grew a widening black crevice. Suddenly the shield shattered, and it was jettisoned from the ship in large chunks. The men inside felt the lurch, then saw the threatening hole. The gray alloy gave way then, allowing the small pocket of air to burst into countless tiny shards of metal and dust.

And the second one:

> The magician could see through the glass-walled case that was to become his watery coffin. Upside down, he could do nothing to stop the liquid from draining into his nose, clogging his windpipe. He desperately tried to remember the formula for escape: Push the pin to

> one side, disengage, flip, and I'm out. But the pin was stuck. He grew dizzy as the water continued to fill his body, bloating his stomach, chest, and face. He was totally confined to this oxygenated but airless box, cut off from life itself. Nearly one and a half minutes had passed, and his body writhed in pain, his lungs and brain fighting each other for air, seconds ticking him away, into the dark. His heart beat, furious, slowing, as the blood simply ceased to pump. The color of the red drapes around the tank turned to a dark, muted black.

I read over them again. I felt after I wrote them that they were missing something, but I didn't know how to explain what it was. Now I can say, I think. In all this death, what's missing, interestingly, oddly, is life. Then I get an idea for a third. I rake through the drawers and find a piece of loose-leaf. I write, for the first time in months, since, really, Fleur:

> It had been hours, and the man could still see a faint outline of the iceberg. He felt as if his blood were coagulating—

(I heard that word in the hospital, when they were explaining to Becky why my cuts hadn't been effective.)

> —coagulating *inside* his body, its color fading into the whiteness of ice. His mind subconsciously told him that his raw muscles were becoming only frozen masses of tissue, unable to move. The calm but refrigerated water seemed to churn around him as he tried to relax in his life jacket. Ice was already causing the orange material to crack and tear, and he knew that it would give way, allowing the ice to penetrate his

> clothes to numb his flesh, indifferent to the fact that he would die in storage and be preserved here forever. As his body surrendered to the stunning cold, he became one with the iceberg that was just disappearing into the gloom.

I read over it, slowly this time, carefully. I find only one phrase that comes close to what I want to say, what I want to feel. "As his body surrendered to the stunning cold . . ." and I want to say he knew he would be dead soon, but I don't change a word. Instead, I feel it, a little. ". . . stunning . . ."

Better, I think. Closer. And I climb back into bed, satisfied enough to sleep.

ELEVEN

When I wake up, I call in to the Metronome and Rich tells me they've hired someone new to take my place until I get myself back together again. I almost ask him what that means.

I sit in bed and think about the dreams. I clearly remember seeing Jason and Barbara, the girl he had the date with, having dinner, then having sex in the shower. But Jason leaves the shower this time, leaving her standing there in a pool of blood, embarrassed but not dead. And then Gary and Sherri in the back seat of his Prelude, or in his parents' bedroom, fucking a Saturday night away. Sherri's breasts wobble inside her T-shirt, and they fall free and swing back and forth when Gary skins the rabbit (as my mom used to say, then my dad later, when he undressed us for bed, the way she used to do) and tosses the shirt to the floor. And she unzips his jeans and pulls off his clothes so slowly, and when she's done, she plays with him, and soon they are thrashing around on the bed, and she is screaming, and her breasts are bouncing all over the room, it seems, Gary's hands on them.

I close my eyes to it, not wanting to see any more, but all

I can see now is Bruce with Richard, doing things to each other I do not want to imagine or see.

When I open my eyes again I expect to see Gary and Sherri still, but it's only Marian, my dream of Marian, and I'm there telling her I don't want to see her again, that it isn't working at all, never will. And she's crying. I can hear her crying, and I put a hand out to feel the tear on her cheek, but just when I touch it, she turns away from me.

"I think you should go and talk to a friend of mine, Deed," Kate says to me later. "She's a psychiatrist. She conducts a workshop for people who've tried to commit suicide."

"How did *you* meet her?" is the only response I can think of. I look around the room, the kitchen, at all these familiar things. The breakfast dishes are still on the table, on top of the morning paper, I forgot to clear them away. Kate's teacup is just one more to do, no problem.

"I talk to her once a week alone, then again with the others," she says, and I keep quiet because I think I know what's coming. She says something else, that she tried to drown herself a year ago, and that's why she goes to see this doctor.

"You?" I say.

She nods, then smiles, looking me right in the eyes. I think I'll have to turn away from her in a moment, but I don't. I keep looking at her. I suddenly want to know why.

"I was very depressed," she says then, without my asking. "I wasn't sure I wanted to keep living. I used to have a house, with a pool in the yard. One night, one night in February, I decided to try it because there just wasn't anything I could see to do besides that. I put on an old fur I'd gotten in Paris when my husband was alive, and I tied a leather belt around myself, around the fur. I wrote my daughter a short note and told her how much I loved her and the kids, and Ray, and I went outside in the rain and jumped into the deep end. You can probably figure out what happened to the fur; it got very heavy, which was the whole idea, and I sank to the bottom. I can't tell you how long I was under, but eventually I decided that what I was doing was wrong, and I began to fight my way back up to the air. The coat was so heavy, and I was terrified that I would die before I made it. But I got there, by God, I got there. I climbed out of the pool and took off that damned coat and threw it away. The very next day I called a real estate agent because I knew I had to get out of that house, and Carolyn, and I told her I wanted to come in and talk to her. I'd met her once at a party, I think, and we had gone out for lunch one day. She seemed very sweet, and I knew about her group. That was for me, I knew. I've been seeing her twice a week for a year now. And I think you should talk to her. You'll like her, you'll like her a lot, and the group is terrific. There aren't many of us, just four—no, three."

I listen, not taking my eyes off her the whole time. I can't see her doing that. Her face is so full of life, this way, now. I ask her why, and she says she'll tell me someday, not now. Then she asks me again about seeing the doctor.

"I'm not sure."

"Look, darling," she says. Lately, she's been calling me that. "It can't hurt. It's too soon for you to know, but it's very hard to come back, once you've failed to do it."

"What do you mean?"

"I mean, it's hard to get back into living again. It's hard to adjust for a while, to get back in the swing of things. You'll see what I mean."

"I think I'm okay," I say, and for a second, I believe it. Then, the paragraphs, the dreams, the questions. "Sort of."

"Sort of, right. All I want you to do is talk to her, one

time. If you hate it, that's okay, but you won't hate it, I promise you. You'll like it, it helps. She makes it easier."

I smile at her, she smiles back.

She says, "I'll call her for you," and she puts her hand over mine. I turn mine over and hold hers. It's cold.

Looking down at them, I say, "Okay."

One afternoon when I was fifteen, my dad asked me what I was doing Saturday. Jason was in Mississippi with his folks for a family reunion. His whole family was really into all that stuff, in exactly the same way I used to wish mine was. But that was impossible from the start, and especially now, with my mom gone. Her mother, my grandmother, never got along with my father, said he was "a man," which for her was a bad thing to be, even for a man. She never trusted men too much. So now they don't talk at all, which leaves Becky and me without a grandmother, sort of. But that's got nothing to do with this.

After I told Dad I had no plans, he took me into the living room. He sort of let himself fall into his big chair, like always, and I sat cross-legged on the floor near him. He asked me why I didn't go out on dates, if I had ever kissed a girl.

No, I told him, I hadn't kissed anyone. And as for dates, I didn't know how to answer him. I was fifteen and a half that winter, and only a few guys were dating, mostly the jocks, and they only dated the cheerleaders. If you weren't a jock, you could kiss your weekends goodbye, especially at Newman, I knew, but also, to a point, at Franklin, where I was by then.

"Don't you *want* to go out?" he asked.

"Sure I do. It's just . . ." How do you tell your father you're afraid of girls? (Of certain rejection, to tell the truth.)

"Look, Walt, it's no big deal, it's just I want you to start having some fun, and I want you to begin having the kind of . . . experiences you should."

"Experiences?"

"Yeah. I think it's about time I took you downtown, don't you think?"

"Why?" I knew why, but the less he knew about what I knew, the better.

"Walt, you're not . . . are you?"

Oh, gay. A faggot. "No, Dad."

"Then what's the problem? Aren't you curious about women? Boy, when I was fourteen, I'd already screwed maybe three girls. Don't you think about that?"

"Sure, a lot, but—"

"Okay then, this weekend, tomorrow, we'll go down and have some fun," my father said. I knew he was only trying to be a dad, but . . .

"With a hooker?"

"With a hooker." He nodded.

"Do we have to?"

" 'Do we *have* to?' Don't you *want* to?"

"Well, not really."

"I thought you said you weren't a . . ."

"I'm not. But I don't want to go downtown and screw some girl I don't know. I want to . . . I want to feel something," I said. "Isn't that what it's all about? Love?"

"Yeah, but you have to understand something about sex, Walt. There's more to it than love. That's only one part of it. There's also know-how," he said, leaning forward.

I think he saw my face, so he went on with it. "What happens when you love someone, and you discover you want to make love to her? What do you do?"

"You want me to tell you?"

"Sure."

". . . I don't know. You just make love, that's all."

"That's what I mean. Women are very special people. And you have to know what you're doing, how to please them. And the best way to learn how to please a woman is to practice, to have some experiences with them. So I think it'd be a good idea to learn a little this weekend."

"What about the first time?" I asked.

"What about it?" he said.

"Isn't it supposed to be special?"

"For girls it is, sure."

"What about for boys? For me?"

"Forget it. It's your job to make sure you do the right thing, and the people who can teach you how to do it are downtown."

"But they're whores, Dad, not teachers," I argued.

"They're *women,* Walt. They know what works and what doesn't."

"Okay," I said, "that's fine. But I don't want my first time to be just a fuck"—his face drained when I said the word—"just a fuck somewhere in the Quarter. I want to love someone first."

"But—"

"No, Dad. I understand what you're saying about learning and experiences, but look, if I love a girl and she loves me, then isn't it better if we learn about love and sex together?"

"No," he said, and I could tell he was getting frustrated and angry at all this. I could see in his face he knew I was gay; from where he was sitting, I guess I must have *looked* gay. I wished he could see I wasn't. But he went to Newman, too . . .

Then he changed his voice. He said, "When I was a boy, your granddad took me over to some woman's house on the other side of the Quarter, and he paid her to teach me. Shit, Walt, I didn't even know her name. She was tall, she had red hair, and huge tits. And she took me to bed for three days straight."

My dad looked away, leaned back in the chair. His eyes fixed on the wall, like he was watching a movie of himself banging the nameless, red-haired cunt his father bought him one weekend.

"I'll tell you, Walt," he said after a few minutes, "it was something else. *She* was something else. By the end of the second day, I knew everything I wanted to know, and more. I'd touched things I'd only dreamed about before, I'd kissed things I never knew existed. In the end, I was taking *her* back to bed, lemme tell you." My dad smiled at me, and I waited for him to wink, and I was happy when he didn't.

Eventually, we went downtown to some place off Bourbon, and some tall blond woman took me by the hand and led me upstairs to a small room filled with a king-sized bed. I was only in there for the night, and the whole time, there were sounds coming through the walls—the sounds of sex.

She fucked me over and over, her mouth on my mouth, her mouth around my dick, her hands between her legs, and then between mine, her tits in my mouth, then wrapped around my dick, and my goo (as I called it when I was fifteen and a half) in her mouth, on her breasts, on her hands, and all over both of us, and everywhere.

My dad was right: I did learn. I even enjoyed it. But still, I regret it.

The next time I had a girl undressed beside me was when I was dating Frankie. My dad had said I'd be hungry for it after that night, and he was right about that, too. But I waited for love, or what I thought was love—for Frankie.

Now, when I think about her, I see that it was only fucking, that love hadn't come yet. It still hasn't. The strange thing is, even though I do a lot of fucking, now that I have Marian at my disposal, all I want is to love. And to make love.

I used to wish for someone to understand. A woman, really. I knew one who would have, but before I was old enough to talk to her about it, or to know I would want to, she died. I wonder if my dad thinks about her, too. Or dreams about her, the way I do, when it rains, and when I think of Destin.

I've pretty much put that night of fucking out of my mind, because if I think about it too much, it only upsets me. I always felt that if my mom had been there, she would have stopped him from taking me down there, to that. These days, with Marian and with my one-night stands, it feels exactly the same. Fucking isn't, mustn't be, all there is to sex. There has to be something more. Once in a while, I ask myself why I keep doing it if I don't like it. One answer is that I *do* like it. I'm no fool. After that's out in the open, there's only one answer available to me, which is that it doesn't matter, it doesn't hurt anyone, at least I hope it doesn't. Like gunning with Chip in his Mustang, or like dancing with Marian at some dark club, fucking has become something to do. Meaningless, mindless fun. Nothing more.

After dinner, when I close my eyes, I wait to see the pictures of Jason, or Chip, or whoever, again. Or for the first time, the whore. I wonder, if I keep them closed much longer, which face I'll see. What will I dream? I decide that if I can just see Kate every once in a while, I won't need to worry about it, or see the doctor. Maybe I'll dream about Kate. Or my mother.

TWELVE

Kate calls in the morning and tells me I am penciled in for after lunch. By the time she calls, my sister has left for the airport, to return to school in Pennsylvania, and my dad has left for work. There is no one to talk with about how nervous I am at the thought of meeting and talking to this new woman.

I'm nervous because I know I'll have to talk about it again today. Not again, really, it will only be the second time, but not even my family has heard about it. I know that everyone who knows me wants to know what happened, exactly what happened. *I* would, if some guy I knew had done it, or tried to.

As I pull the front door shut, the phone rings, and I think a moment before going back inside to answer it. I hope strongly that I have been erased, postponed until tomorrow. I will be ready tomorrow. More ready, anyway.

I answer. Here we go.

"Are you all right?" Becky and I have always been close, though more recently than when we were younger; she tells me now that she just couldn't get on the plane without making sure I was okay. Funny, she'd been here several days, yet we hadn't had a chance to sit down and talk. About anything.

Becky has always been as pushy, though, as she is today. She goes about it in funny ways sometimes, but she usually gets what she wants. The thing I admire about her is that she isn't afraid of anything, never has been. She always has questions, and she's not afraid to ask them. She once said to me, "Deed, the one thing I wish I could change about you is that you don't ask enough questions. You're too satisfied with the usual answers. You have to start going after what you want, asking questions about the things you want to know, doing what it takes to get what you want."

I once asked her why she lied so much. She told me her lies don't harm anyone, that she uses the truth to do and get what she wants. That that's how the most successful people do it, and she wants to be like them. I guess maybe it's a gift, like singing.

My gift, I guess, is still to be decided. Maybe it's patience.

Another time, I told her during a fight I thought her favorite question was "Why?"

Her answer to that remark startled me so much that the fight ended, I even forgot what we were fighting about, and I started immediately to think about myself more, about what I wanted, and about what I could do to get it.

What she said was "No, Deed, you're wrong." She smiled at me, and said, "*Your* favorite question is 'Why?' My favorite question is 'Why not?' "

Today, on the phone, this is one of the times I wish she'd leave it, me, alone. But I know it's a lost battle, that an answer is what she wants.

"Yeah, but look, I really don't want to get into it now. I'm on my way out."

"Where to so early?"

"The doctor, a friend of Kate's," I tell her.

"That lady?"

"Yeah," I say.

"What for? Is she a shrink?"

"Yeah, a shrink," I say, thinking that's just what I need to hear now, thanks loads.

"She's gonna make you talk, you know, they always do," Becky tells me.

"Maybe, maybe not. It's just to meet her, anyway," I say, trying to defend what has become my position and not only Kate's. I wait a few seconds, but Becky says nothing, and I know she is waiting to hear it all now, because how can I tell a perfect stranger everything if I can't tell my sister? But what she doesn't understand is that Carolyn's being a perfect stranger might make it easier, that's what Kate said.

I know if one of us doesn't say something I'm going to hang up, so I tell her everything, everything at once, because that's how I felt at the time, all at once in about two minutes, the *Reader's Digest* version of my attempt at suicide. In retrospect, I think doses of it would have been better.

No, it wasn't an accident.

I tried to kill myself, yes.

Yes, I'm sure (razor blades do not habitually insert themselves into the wrists of young men).

And Becky says she doesn't understand my tone. I have this habit of being glib when I should be serious. But after you've gone and fucked up a pretty simple suicide, it's hard to be serious about it, I try to tell her, thinking, Fuck you and fuck my tone. There are some things meant to be laughed at.

I leave the very empty house again and walk over to the stand for this week's *Newsweek.* I'm a day late, I should have picked it up yesterday, but it slipped my mind. Roy sees me coming and says, "You're late, Deed."

"I know," I say. "Sorry."

"Yeah. Listen," he says as I walk up, "they shipped us too few this week, so . . ."

"You mean you're sold out?"

"Yeah, sold out, sorry."

I look at Roy closely for a few seconds, thinking he probably heard and thought saving my issue would be pointless, seeing how I was either dead or too screwed up to read. Then I say, "It's okay. Next week."

"F'sure, no sweat," Roy says.

I glance down at the headlines on the day's papers. I have been out of touch, it seems to me, for longer than just a few days. All the headlines say the same thing, more or less, the *Times-Picayune,* the New York *Times,* and *USA Today:* SHUTTLE EXPLODES; SEVEN KILLED.

I close my eyes a moment and try to remember the teacher, her face. It comes to me, and I feel a chill inside, an emptiness, like the one I felt when I found out Frankie's brother died long before I had a chance to meet him. I feel a loss, I guess, because they're other people, the teacher and the others, I will surely never meet, no matter what. *Dammit.*

I walk away into the sunlight, a new face among those already in my mind pictures, and I shield my eyes against the glare.

Carolyn's office is in a building near the hospital, a white building on Dryades. The white lobby has a fountain in the center and large paintings of clouds on the wall . . . I walk through to the stand in the back to get a *Newsweek,* but they're sold out, too. There's a fresh stack of *Life,* though, the "Year in Pictures" issue.

In the elevator, it occurs to me that perhaps Carolyn

"pencils" people in because there's always a doubt about whether they'll actually be around to attend the next meeting. I'm fifteen minutes early, which will give me plenty of time to leaf through the copy of *Newsweek* she should have in her waiting room. As I walk down the hallway toward her office, I can see the lobby below. The hallway is a balcony, and you can look over the side, straight down. I think this is an unwise place for a psychiatrist to have her office, especially one who deals with people . . . like me. Who knows? For some attempted suicides, trying it might be like eating chocolate; it comes in cravings. The temptation of this fifth-floor balcony might prove fatal. I stop a second and look over. I can see the man in the stand smoking a cigarette, and I think that maybe she put her office here on purpose as a way to help them, us, build strength.

Then again, maybe not.

The waiting room is filled with grossly stuffed furniture and huge, drooping plants. The room is empty, but it seems crowded even so, with this stuff. I try one of the safer-looking chairs, but I sink into it nearly to the floor, swallowed really, my balance lost. I look around to see if anyone is hidden, watching, then over at the frosted glass of the receptionist's window. I'm glad it's closed.

On the white walls are framed paintings. A sailboat scene, a farm scene, a group-of-children-playing scene, a glider-among-the-clouds scene. I wonder how much she paid for these scenes and decide it was too much. But they certainly fit the furniture, and before I knock on the frosted glass, I decide the doctor better have several ingredients her waiting room lacks. One last look around, then I struggle out of the chair to the floor, so I can find my balance and stand up.

When I tell the receptionist who I am, she tells me I will be seen at once because the one-thirty didn't show. I consider asking if the one-thirty was penciled in and then erased due to some unforeseen complication, like too strong a temptation or something. But I don't because I promised Becky I would try and control my glibido.

Carolyn looks just as I thought she would; Kate's description was right on the money: tall, but not too; not pretty, but attractive ("You'll see what I mean," said Kate, and I do); auburn hair; green eyes; beautiful smile. Ann-Margret came to Kate's mind, and comes to mine, too.

She tells me to call her Carolyn, not Dr. Moore (though I have never heard her last name until now), because "Dr." would put a distance between us. She wants us to be friends. I come just to the edge of asking her why I have to pay her when I have other friends who would gladly get the whole story out of me for free.

We begin.

"Can I ask a question?"

"Of course," she says, and I like the way it sounds, her answering me.

"Why am I here?"

She looks at me from the side of her face, her eyes squinted. She slowly turns to face me and says, "You're here so we can talk."

"About . . . ?"

"You. Me. Life." She waits a moment, then: "Death. Anything at all, really, whatever you want."

"Anything I want?"

"Sure. Ask me a question, another one, a good one."

"Why do you want to talk to me?" I ask.

"Because Kate said I would enjoy it."

"You enjoy talking to people who've tried to kill themselves?"

"I think 'enjoy' is the wrong word for it. I do it because it's my work, and I love my work," she says. "Besides, I hope we can talk about more than suicide. Kate says you're pretty special."

I don't expect that, and after a second, I ask, "Why do you do this? Why are you a psychiatrist?"

"The truth?"

I nod.

She says, "Because my mother died in childbirth and I never knew her, and it's always . . . bothered me, and I want to know why."

"Why what?" I ask.

"Why everything," she says, right into my eyes.

Suddenly I am nervous. Her eyes on me are powerful. Something tells me she's in control, though she's letting me think I am. (And I feel that I am.) She's letting me test her. Smart woman, I think; I like her.

"Do you want me to tell you why I did what I did?" I ask.

"Yes," right into my eyes again. She means it.

"Not today," I tell her. "Another time."

"Good. Any other questions, Deed?" She looks away from me, down to a pack of cigarettes on her desk, Camels, and a lighter. She shakes a cigarette out and puts it to her lips and inhales deeply, without lighting. I've never seen anything like this before.

Even though I feel as though I have now given up my chance to ask any other questions, I say, "Are you going to light that?"

"No, I inhale them dry, it's healthier."

I ask, "Then what's the lighter for?"

She looks up at me now and says, "In case I get weak."

"Like having your office on the fifth floor of this building, with that hallway."

She smiles. I smile back. We understand each other.

"Do you get weak often?"

"No, not too often," she says, still smiling. Kate was

right. Beautiful smile. I think I would like to see it again sometime.

"How many patients do you have?"

"Not too many, just a few. There's Kate, and Jane, for a while, and Molly. And maybe you. That's all."

"That's it? Three?"

"That's all. Why so surprised?"

"I guess I thought there'd be more." I look out the window. A block away, on St. Charles, there's a streetcar in front of the drugstore. It's packed, stopped at a red light.

"How many times a week should I come here?" I want to know.

"Once alone, once in group, at least. More if you want, and I suggest a lot more at the beginning. We all meet once a week together to tell stories, to reveal fears, to help each other get through it."

"Get through what?"

"Living."

I look at her a minute, thinking whether or not I'll be able to talk to her the way she wants me to. I suddenly feel the same way I do when Marian asks me to tell her I love her. It's almost the same here, but not quite, because I know soon enough that I *can* talk to Carolyn, that there will be no problems with her at all. I tell her that I like her, just as Kate said I would.

"I like you, too," and another smile. "Before you decide to start seeing me, though, I think you should know that this program is having problems. Reynolds Center wants to shut me down."

I ask why.

"I set up the Suicide Counseling Group to help people deal with coming back after trying to commit. That part has worked well in all cases but one. It's been very successful, especially with people like Kate. My patients handle

being here very well, no problems. *My* problem is that I am becoming obsolete. My patients are doing so well that the Board thinks I am no longer needed, at least in this capacity. What they don't see is that we are a family now, old patients, new patients, and me, and I can't just stop seeing them due to a lack of funds."

"Lack of funds?"

"This program is funded through a grant. It's free to whoever needs it. I just wish we could get more people in here. They're out there, we know that, and I'm beginning to think we should do something to get them in here *before* they commit, not after, assuming they fail."

I think, This is interesting. It turns out that here is someone—maybe even a friend—who'll get the story for free after all. Eventually.

"So you might disappear one day?"

"Not quite. But the free treatment will end, and that will present a big problem for people like Kate and Molly, who don't have a lot of money. But all this is months away, not close enough to panic over. I just thought you should know."

"I still want to see you. It doesn't matter about all that. If I have to stop seeing you for a while, I guess I'll handle it. I think I've had it with suicide."

"Good, and thank you. Now, I have a question for you. Where did your name come from?"

"I made it up," I tell her. It's the truth. "My real name is Walter, which isn't a bad reason on its own. But anyone can be a Walter Smith. I didn't want to be *anyone,* so I changed it, I became Deed."

"Why that name, why Deed?"

I smile now, happy that she is intrigued over my name. "When I chose the word," I say, "I didn't really know the reason. I mean, I knew it in my head, I just didn't know the words. After my mother was killed, I realized—and I was

still pretty young—that I wanted more control over things, over my life. I didn't know how to say that, either."

"Your mother was killed. How?"

"In an accident."

"Will you talk about it with me sometime?"

"I'll have to think about it, okay?" She nods, smiles, knowing somehow. "My father, he's a real estate agent, so I knew all his talk, the buzzwords, from being around it all the time. So when I decided to change my name, in high school, I knew I wanted something different. I chose Deed because it was like buying a house, sort of, like getting me, like finally *owning* me. I gave myself ownership of my own life, I guess. I took control, and responsibility."

"I like that," Carolyn says.

I realize it all sounds pretty damn good out loud.

"I have one more question, Deed, before I let you go. What you tried to do, was that taking control of your life, too? Was that taking responsibility?"

Her eyes remain on mine. I look away, behind her, to the wall. There's a photograph, a black-and-white, of a woman. It must be her mother when she was very young; she looks about eighteen or nineteen. There's also a framed print on the wall; it's a thin woman sort of reclining on her side in a field of golden wheat, and there's a house and a barn or something in the distance. It looks familiar, but not enough to mean anything.

I stand up and grab my jacket and walk to the door under the EXIT sign, not the door I came in through, and open it, thinking maybe I was wrong about her, and I see the long hallway, and the edge of the balcony, and one edge of the highest cloud painting, and I turn around and look back at her, trying to think of the answer. I can see another wall from here. On it is a large tapestry, probably from Africa. It looks African. Next to it is a framed poster. Written in fancy print are four lines. Below the lines it says, "William Wordsworth, 1770–1850." The four lines are:

> Though nothing can bring back the hour
> Of splendor in the grass, of glory in the flower;
> We will grieve not, rather find
> Strength in what remains behind . . .

Right away I look at Carolyn's face. Her eyes are still on mine, and I see in her face that she has seen me reading the lines, that I know what they mean. I look back at them once more, at "We will grieve not, rather find strength in what remains behind," and suddenly I see my face reflected in the glass. And then I say, "No," then I look at Carolyn, then: "I don't know," and leave, shutting the door.

"Can I talk to you?" I ask Kate a few hours later, at a restaurant near Carolyn's.

"Of course," Kate says. She is a little tired from her walk from the streetcar stop a few blocks away. Even though it's after noon, and winter, the sun drains us all, mostly those Kate's age. When she's tired like this, it's the only time her age shows so strongly, so frighteningly.

I tell Kate about Marian, the problem that after a year, all I want is to get away from her, somehow. "I even had a dream about it a couple of nights ago," I say. I tell her we sleep together often, and that I knew she liked me, right from the start, and Kate picks up her glass of iced tea and sucks some through the straw, avoiding my eyes for the first time. "I know what you're thinking," I say. "You're thinking that I've been using her for sex, right?" But Kate doesn't answer, which *is* her answer, and I know it. I know it mostly because *I* have been thinking so, too. Just being horny isn't enough, I know that, and I say it, partly so Kate knows I know it, partly so I can hear it. But now that it's happened, I say, I don't know what to do.

Kate has no answers for me. She changes the subject when I am done, and I am disappointed. I suppose she is, too.

Before we get up to leave, I ask, "What do you think I should do about Marian?"

Kate looks at me as if to say she thought we were all through with that, but after a moment, she says, "I think you need to think about it. I don't know what you should do. *Should* really has nothing to do with it anymore, Deed. What's done is done. Maybe you better not do anything right now. Just let things be, and see what happens." She smiles a little at me, which tells me she feels a little better having said her piece. We leave then, and for a few minutes, I watch her walk back to the streetcar stop, in the setting sun. Before she gets there and turns around, I walk away so she won't see me.

I watch the Mardi Gras parade over on Louisiana. By the time I get there, it's dark. This is my first parade this year. The best ones aren't for days, and Mardi Gras itself is still more than a week away, but I can sure use the yelling tonight. They don't throw much, not this early in the season.

I remember spending Mardi Gras with Jason last year. He was the only person I ever knew who wore costumes to every parade. At the very least, some weird makeup on his face. Last year, his best one was a zombie. He had a long green coat with a large hood, and he put gray-green makeup all over his face and hands, which made his fingers look even longer than usual, and sinister. All day long, he sort of lurched around, and by the time we went to the Quarter to see the girls on the balconies flashing their tits, his satin bag was filled with carnival beads and trinkets and doubloons. A zombie, no less!

As I watch, a float goes by covered with red devils. I look around at all the people, but there aren't too many out tonight, not compared with the crowds that'll be out for the parades later this week, and next. For some reason, all I can think about is the last time I saw Jason. It was the day before he died, and he was all excited about his big date with Barbara. He told everyone about it. She was his dream, his ticket into the powerful group of guys from school. All of them wanted to get that first date with her, but she wouldn't even talk to them; she hadn't when we were in school, no reason to out, I guess. And then Jason gets this date with her. It was his only way in, and everybody knew it, too, maybe even Barbara. He promised he'd call and let me know how it went when he got home.

On Saturday afternoon, one of the guys told me he saw Jason at Katz and Besthoff buying rubbers. He thought it was great, this guy.

"I can't believe this guy," this guy said to me. "That little prick's gonna get into her pants before any of us!"

I said, "So? That's good, isn't it?"

"Damn right!" he said.

"You know he wants to be in with you guys," I said.

"Yeah, I know. This'll get him in, Deed. We're all getting together at Cooter's later, after we see him with her."

"See him with her?" *See him with her?*

"He's taking her out for dinner. We're all meeting him at the Butterfly to get some of the action," he said.

I looked at him, that sex-hungry, half-broken-out face. The shit's probably a virgin, can't find a girl dumb enough to slice that pizza, I thought. Standing there, I knew they'd kill it for him, they'd push him into it, then fuck it up and laugh about it, and Jase'd be nowhere again. "Stay away from it, for Pete's sake. Can't you just leave him alone and let him have some fun?"

"Fuck off! Jason knows all about it. One of us'll be at her house, watching her leave with him. Then another at the restaurant, I forget where. Then he's taking her to the 'Fly to fuck her, and at midnight, we're all meeting him there and we're going for it. We're gonna gang her," he said to me in a low voice.

"And then what, asshole?"

"And then your pal's *in,* Deed-o, which is something you'll never be, faggot."

"Fuck you," I said.

That night, I tried to get him on the phone, but there wasn't any answer. Then around eight-thirty he called and said to come over. He said she'd stood him up and that it was all over. "She fucked me over," that's how he said it. He sounded okay, though, just like always, more or less, certainly not like he was thinking of strangling the life out of himself. I told him I'd take him to the Grill to celebrate, and he laughed.

I got to his house around nine, but when I knocked, no one answered. After a while, I tried the door, but it was locked. I knew he was in there because I could hear the stereo, so I banged on the door. And it swung open.

The stereo was blasting the new Wham! tune, and all I could think was to turn the damned thing off. I knew where his room was, of course, so I went upstairs to find him. His door was open. I went in, and all his stuff was everywhere, like he had ripped the room apart. Books and clothes and broken records and shit all over the place; there was pile of shattered records in a corner, like he Frisbeed a dozen of them against the wall and let the shards fly. Unbelievable scene. I hit the power button on the stereo, cutting off Sting's "If You Love Somebody Set Them Free" right at the start. Then all I could hear was water, running water. At first I didn't know where it was coming from.

After that, everything happened fast, but in slow motion. Like, one picture, one frame, at a time. I saw steam coming out of the bathroom; the door wasn't closed all the way. I pushed it open. The first thing I saw was Jason's face on top of a body that looked like a rag doll, dropped. His eyes were open, and his left hand was behind his head, like he was rubbing his neck.

"Jase," I said. I almost apologized for being late, but then I saw the rope around his neck, and my throat closed up. The cockeyed angles of his position on the floor, I saw that. The blood on the carpet and in the shower, where his legs were, still. The ill color of his bloated face, the blood on his mouth, and in his eyes, where the whites should have been.

I ran out of the room, back into the bedroom, and I tripped over a bureau drawer. From the floor, I could see him in the bathroom. He didn't move. I crawled back in and touched his right arm, shook it a little. It was icy, even in the steamy room. His body fell over onto the floor. His mouth fell open and I thought he was screaming, but it was me.

I stood up and looked in the shower. Part of the rope was still inside, swirling around in the water under his legs as it spun into the drain. The fibers were pink-stained, with patches of white. I shut off the water. For a long time, drips hit the drain and his leg, counting the seconds away . . .

I caught my face in the mirror, but it was all blurred in the steam. I couldn't make out any features. Just the soft outline of my face and upper body, and a clear image of Jason's face, his eyes wide, on the floor, framed in a steamless section near the bottom, where the mist had burned off. I couldn't take my eyes from his. When I finally closed them, it did no good; all I could see was Jason's face, screaming and dead. After a while, I went down and called the police.

THIRTEEN

I have an appointment with Carolyn this morning. I have decided to see her regularly, at least for now. I'm early, so I walk over to the Emergency Room at Reynolds Center, on Marengo. I guess I'm drawn there, probably because that's where they said they were bringing Jason that night.

It isn't crowded, but a few minutes after I sit down, they wheel a stretcher in. A boy is laid out on it, a small black boy. Right behind them come the boy's parents, and his mother is crying, but not loudly. She is dressed in a shiny brown print dress, tied at the waist. Her head is covered with a bandanna, and the ends of pink curlers poke out at the edges. Many of her teeth, mostly at the front, are capped in gold. Her husband is tall, huge, a lifter. Probably works on the docks, over at Avondale. At least one of his teeth is gone, leaving a hole in the line of toothpaste-commercial white in his mouth. His hands could break a log like a pencil. His green T-shirt is ripped in one spot, his blue jeans are caked in dusty dirt, and his work shoes look centuries old, yet were most likely bought new last week.

I sit up to see more of the boy, but they wheel him

directly into the treatment area, which is through a set of double wooden doors, separate. A yuppied-up woman, a doctor, comes out after a few minutes to talk to the parents.

"Good morning, I'm Jane Weller, the physician on duty," I hear her say. She walks them over to a desk with a white Formica top, and she takes a pile of papers from a drawer. Now they are too far away for me to hear, but they begin to fill out the papers. The doctor walks away, back into the treatment area.

The parents fill in only a couple of spaces on the forms. The doctor comes back out, and they all talk, still too far away for me to hear. I see the towering man shake his head a couple of times, then they talk some more. Actually, the doctor does most of the talking, and she wipes her brow many times while she speaks. I want to move closer so I can hear, but I stay put because I don't want to be kicked out. For the first time, I notice the smell of medicine, that clean but irritating antiseptic odor.

The woman starts to cry again, and then a red-haired man in white walks out of the treatment area and over to the doctor. He pulls her aside and whispers something to her, and her face falls and loses all its color; the man in white goes back into the treatment area. I look back at the doctor, and now her face is close to the color of Chip's that last day at the Grill, but this woman is white to begin with. The doctor turns toward me, and she wipes her face with her sleeve again, then looks right at me, as if she knows I've been thinking about her and watching all this. Then she goes back to the boy's parents and says something, and the next thing I hear is the mother's crying, loud now, and her hands are up over her face, and the word "died." That's all, just that word, no others. I look away from all of them, at the floor, then at the swinging doors which lead to the treatment area, "died," and then I get up slowly and walk out into the warm February daylight, over to Carolyn's office.

When she asks me what's wrong, I'm not sure what to say. "A little boy just died," maybe, but no. "I'm beginning to have second thoughts," maybe, but no. I don't know right now. I say that.

"Tell you what," she says, leaning forward in her chair. She takes a cigarette out of the pack and sucks on it, dry. "Just talk and maybe it'll come out."

"I don't get it," I say.

"Just talk. It's like answering a question you don't know the answer to. If you answer it any old way, there's a chance it could be the right answer, see?"

"No," I say, "but go on, anyway."

"Well, if your answer's wrong"—dry drag—"you'll probably know it. *I* would, if it were me. So then you give a different answer, and you keep going until you find the right one."

"I get it. Lie for a while . . ."

"Until you find the truth."

I nod.

"Look," she says, putting the cigarette down, "let's just say that the phrase 'I don't know' is banned from this discussion. You *have* to give me an answer. If you can't think of one, then make it up. It'll be wrong, but it may show us the way to the right one. Okay?"

"I guess," I say, though not at all sure this isn't bogus bullshit.

"Good. Now, what's the matter, Deed?" She leans back in her chair, waiting for some kind of revelation from me.

I sit there for a few minutes, silent, thinking. I look around her office. For the first time, I notice a sculpture on one of the walls, a thing with millions of colors on it. I get up and go over to it, but by the time I get there, it's changed. I walk back and forth a couple of times, my eyes on it, watching it change. "That's great," I say.

"It was made by a man named Agam," she says.

"Agam?"

"Yaacov Agam. He's from Israel. What's the matter, Deed?"

"Why is it so important to you?" I ask, not turning back to her yet.

"What are you trying to hide? Why is your image so important?"

"What image?"

"That tough-guy, insensitive, decadent image. You want everyone to think you're so far away from them so badly you don't know where you really are. You know what I'm talking about."

"So?" I sit back down.

"So why do you do it? And why here?"

"Why not? I mean, you have to. To survive. I spent my whole goddamned childhood being walked all over, because I was different, openly different, and little boys are cruel to you if you're different. After enough years, you develop a shell. Only certain things get through."

"Why?"

"What the fuck is with you, Carolyn? Why? Because it takes too much energy to be tied up with every little thing. It's too tiring to be depressed all the time. You just have to turn off sometimes, you know? You have to . . . relax sometimes. *I* have to." I am pacing the room, combing my hair with my fingers, and Carolyn is sitting up in her chair.

For just a moment I glance at her face, at her eyes, then at the rest. What kind of woman is she? Is she married? Does she have any children? I look over at her desk, and there are no photos of children there—only one, of an elderly man, too old to be her husband. Where did Carolyn come from? She's not from here, she doesn't act like she's from here; she's too . . . fast. She's obviously got some money somewhere, because she can afford to do this counseling in a free program; her grant can't be much, certainly not as much as she *could* get, somewhere else. I look back at the man on her desk—her father, because, I remember now, her mother is dead. *There's* a small item we have in common. I wonder, did having no mother do things to her, as it did to me? She said her mother died in childbirth, so Carolyn never even knew her. At first, I think that must have been particularly hard. On the other hand, though, can you miss something you never had? Can a person blind from birth *miss* a sunset over Lake Pontchartrain, the way I would if I went blind tomorrow? When I was growing up, did I miss having friends? No, I didn't, because I chose not to have them, and I never knew what having them was like; much later, I realized that, as the saying goes, I didn't know what I was missing. I must remember, I tell myself, to ask Carolyn about missing her mother. I look back at her, at the eyes, green, like trees.

"I ask again," she says, "what's bothering you?"

"I don't know!!" *Fucking frustrating bitch!*

"We made a deal—"

"*Fuck* your deal!! That's the problem! I just don't know anymore!" I say.

She waits a second. Then, quietly: "What do you mean?"

I take a breath, to loosen the muscles in my face, or try to. "When I was growing up, I knew everything. I always had *the* answer. I knew why I was different. I knew why I didn't want to be just like everybody else. I knew what and who I liked and didn't like, and why. I mean, there wasn't anything I didn't know. I spent my whole fucking childhood alone, going over questions and answers in my mind because you have to do *some*thing, right? I was like Thoreau at Walden Pond! Except for all I knew, I was there *forever,* not just two years. By the time I was thirteen, I knew myself inside and out, up and down, better than some people know themselves their whole lives, better than they *want* to know themselves. You could have asked me anything, and I would have had an answer. Anything! And my answer would have been the right one, too, first time out. None of this bullshit lying to find the truth. But now . . . now, I can't answer everything the way I used to. There's a hell of a lot I don't know. About myself, I mean. And it's only gotten worse since I . . . And it's driving me crazy," I say, sitting down again, "crazy."

"I can imagine," she says softly.

"Yeah, well, if you can, don't. It's not a good time, believe me."

"So the problem is . . . decisions? Choices you have to make?"

"Choices. I guess so. The future, really. It's dark, where it used to be bright. I don't know anymore what's going to happen in a year, two years . . ."

"No one does, Deed. That's part of it," she says.

"Part of what?"

"Living," she says.

"Living. That's not enough," I say. "I want to do more than just live. And I guess, I guess the trouble is that I don't know *how* to do more. I don't see a way to do it. I'm not even sure what I want to do with my life, for God's sake! You see? It's just that. *I don't know.*"

I close my eyes. Darkness. The future, I think. But I look deeper, for some sign of light. "Kate said you'd help me get back into it, living," I say, still peering into the dark. "Is that what we're doing?"

"Yes, *if* that's what I'm doing for you. Am I helping you . . . get back into living?"

"I don't—" I smile, then think about it. "Yes," I say. "You're helping. Can I ask you a question?"

"Sure."

"Do you think I'm a good person?"

"Why do you ask?"

"Just once, I wish you could answer a question without asking one of your own."

"I'm sorry, but it's important."

"When isn't it?"

She sort of shrugs.

"Shit," I say. "I don't— Because *I* don't know if I am or not. I mean, I haven't led the most pristine life. I've done a lot of stuff. Drugs, sex . . ."

"Did you enjoy what you were doing?"

"You mean like sex? I love sex. Don't you?"

"We're still on *your* decadence, not mine," she says, sitting up in her chair again and smiling.

"We'll have to get back to it, then," I say. No response. "I enjoyed it, yeah. And I haven't done a lot of drugs, just pot, mostly, and some coke."

She looks at me closely, squinting her eyes. "Well, *I* think you're a good person, but I don't think it matters much what I think. *You* have to know you're a good person for it to matter."

"I know, I know. It all stems from being different for so long. I use sex and drugs as a way to show them that I'm not *totally* different. The line's not as dark anymore, you know? Not as solid. I mean, if I can show them I'm not as weird as they think I am, then maybe it'll help the situation all around. Maybe it will stop their wondering about who I really am. But I'm afraid of it, too. A big part of me still doesn't want people to see the real me."

"How come?"

"Because I value myself too much to show it to everybody. Do you know what I mean? Is that terrible? In grade school, everybody was so shitty, I just turned off completely. I became someone else when I was in school. It was while I was really into learning about myself, and I found stuff in there, inside me, that I really liked, good things—and I guess I want to show them only to certain people."

"So why do drugs at all? Why do it just for them?"

"Because. Because being different—*that* different—can be really lonely. You turn yourself off to them, so that you become almost deaf to their language, blind to their lives altogether. Then there's only so far you can go before you know everything about yourself, and then you're done, at least for the moment. After that, you have to go outside, out to the others, to the ones who forced you to lock yourself up in the first place. What scares me is that I think I might be too late. Maybe there's no one who really *cares* about knowing the real me."

"The you behind the drugs and sex."

"Yeah."

She squints her eyes again. "How do you know who to show it to? The real you."

I shrug. "I just know."

"Have I seen any of it?"

"Parts. I have a feeling you'll see more."

"You're sure? I mean, I want to, I really do. I want to know the real Deed Smith."

"You will, you will," I say. No one's ever said they wanted to know me before. It feels good to have all this out now. I wonder if she knows I've never explained this to anyone before, and how good a sign that must be.

"Would it embarrass you to talk about sex?"

"I don't know." I look at her a moment, and I feel a sort of involuntary smile occupy my mouth. "Try me."

Now she smiles and looks away from me. "It's not really important. I was just wondering, you say you like sex. Is that something you still do? Do you make love a lot?"

By now her eyes are back on me. "Make love? No, I've

never made love." I wait a moment before saying anything more, looking to see what her face tells me. When I see that she is surprised and waiting, I say, "I've only fucked."

"That was fast."

"It's an easy answer."

"Is there a difference?"

"Totally. Fucking is just fucking. But making love is . . . beautiful. More. At least, I hope so. Is it?"

"Yeah," she says, nodding. "Why do you fuck so much?"

"Because it's . . . something to do, really. It's fun."

"Are you fucking someone now?"

"Marian," I say. "Now, *that* bothers me."

"Told you." She smiles, and big.

"Yeah, you told me. I'll run out and get you a medal. You want to hear about Marian?"

"You kidding?" A quick smile.

"Well, I've been seeing her for about a year. Right away, there was an attraction. She was into pretty kinky stuff, and I was willing to try anything. So we started sleeping together. It was terrific for a while. But now she says she wants a commitment, and all *I* want is . . . nothing. Just to get away. She makes it so claustrophobic, so heavy all the time, and I feel guilty now, whenever I see her. I don't want to hurt her, but I'm running out of patience, and choices, you know?"

We sit there, our eyes not on each other, and I remember saying most of this to Kate just yesterday. My eyes dart around the room, to the Agam, to the Wordsworth, to the woman in the wheat field.

"Mostly," I say, "I feel cramped. I feel like I'm almost lying to her, and to myself. Like I've done something terribly wrong, and now I'm paying the consequences. When we first started going out, I was different. I'm not the same now, not altogether. When I'm with her, I feel like I have to be what I was before, and so I can't wait to leave, to be away from her again so I can be myself. Is that wrong?"

"My advice," she finally says, "is to leave it alone for a while. It's obvious to me that you feel something for her, even if it's only guilt, but it's something. You don't want to hurt her. Don't see her for a while. See how that feels. You might miss her, and that might change everything. You might see her in a new light, after a little bit of time passes. Know what I mean?"

"Yeah, that's what Kate said. I just don't want to feel like I've used her," I say.

Carolyn looks at me closely now, and she smiles slightly. "That makes me feel much better about it, Deed. I don't think you should feel that way, either. Do you think you used her? Or did you maybe use each other for a while?"

I look at her now, and it's easier. Everything is easier, from that one thing she just said. "I guess we used each other, and now, it's like she expects more, and I can't give it to her, so it feels like I'm using her. Right?"

"Sounds good to me. So now that you know that, you can do something about it. Right?"

"Sounds good to me." I look over at the Wordsworth. "That poem over there. I like it."

"I know you do," she says. "So do I."

"It really fits in with everything."

"Explain," she says.

I tell her it fits my childhood, how each day was a little easier to get through because of the day before, and that went on for a while, little by little, until I got strong, strong enough, in the end.

She asks if I was strong the day I tried to kill myself.

I tell her no, right away. For a few minutes, I don't say anything. Then: "I tried to kill myself because I didn't see any way out from behind . . . everything. And because I didn't see any reason to find a way. And because of Jason."

I tell her Jason was my best friend. His screaming face floats up before me again, and suddenly I feel numb and claustrophobic here. I tell her I need to leave.

She says it's okay, she understands, and I walk quickly down the hall to the elevator, then from there out into the sun, where there's space and breeze and no darkness.

While I'm walking, I try to remember the lines, but I can't. I can only remember their message. I try to find a way to be strong, I try to see a way for Jason and Chip to make me stronger. But the answer doesn't come, not right away, like I want it to, fast, and I become determined to find it. I keep walking for a long time, until I walk into the darkness.

I end up at Cooter Brown's after dinner, and Richard is there. We play a few games and I win one, but only because Richard sent the eight ball rolling into a side pocket (he made the shot he was aiming for, too). We go into the other room and have a few beers and cheese fries, which are a sin here, and he tells me he wants to "bop" over to AT Two's. So we get into his bullet CRX ("Point and Shoot," the ads said the summer they came out) and leave the parking lot and turn onto River Road, and he throws a tape in, Phil Collins' "In the Air Tonight," and looks over at me and smiles as he flies it around the bend onto Magazine, and the car holds the ground and I can feel the g's pulling me and I laugh out loud because it feels good right now to be totally helpless, at the mercy of forces that I don't understand, relieved maybe of the responsibility, and Richard guns it to seventy because no one's out tonight, and we reach Henry Clay and make it across on yellow and go one more block to Webster and park in the Perlis lot across the street.

Inside, there's a band playing, and they're not too good, and Richard disappears into the men's room. I walk around and take a look at the band, which sounds like The Cold, but is really just a bad imitation.

There must be a thousand people crammed in here tonight, and the smells of beer and pot are everywhere, blended into something new and oddly sweet. I wonder what Richard is doing in the men's room this long, then I decide I don't want to know, so instead I think about "In the Air Tonight" and how it makes me feel, and how if Jason knew, he'd say I was "toad," as in horny. I look around for a girl. Feeling much too familiar here, now, this way, I know that what I want right now is a girl, any girl, her mouth all over me. I spot a pretty blonde about ten feet away, near the juke, and I walk over to her, thinking twice, pace after pace. She's moving to a song that's on the box, a song only she can hear. I stop thinking, for once, and start to move with her, and she smiles a little without letting her teeth show, just spreading the ends of her mouth, and she takes my hand in hers. She rubs it against her thigh, and I feel it on the way, and she licks her lips, and we go to Richard's car.

As we get to the door, Richard comes up with this guy from the bathroom. "You off to the CRiX, Bubba?" Richard has his cool names for many things, like his car and me. The girl and I climb in back, where there's not even a seat because it's too small and cramped, only a small patch of carpet, and Richard and his fag get in front, which has even less room. As soon as the fag closes the door, the chick starts to lick my neck and ears, and her hands move on my legs, over my jeans. I relax because she seems to know how to handle everything, and soon she has slipped her dress over her head, and she's not wearing anything else, and she takes my jeans off, then my underwear, and I strip my shirt off. It is hot in here, and we are sweaty now, which really turns me on. She pushes me down onto the patch of carpeting, bending me in half, and it's very uncomfortable, but she climbs on top of me. Her hand is on me, and she begins to stroke up and down, and my hands move on her back, to her ass, which feels absolutely beautiful. She kisses me long and hard, plunging her tongue into my mouth, then pushes herself onto me, pumping slowly. She arches her back. I hear sounds from the front seat, and I try to imagine how they have positioned themselves in such a small space, even with the seats all the way up on their tracks and leaned back as far as possible. Then the chick begins to moan loudly herself, and I see that the windows have fogged over. I try to move a little, but she tells me not to, the first words we have shared, so I stop, even though my back is broken now. She begins to move faster, and I can feel wetness on my leg, and it's very hot in here now, and it smells like nothing but sex, that very unmistakable odor, and the girl moves faster and begins to really make noise, nearly screaming, and so is Richard, so is the fag, and then she comes and Richard screams and the fag grunts, and she climbs off me, but lies there, her hand stroking me now. In no time, she has moved around so that she can lick me, and her mouth goes around me now, and it's just as warm and smooth, and her head bobs up and down quickly, and I come, I know I do, though I can't feel it, or anything, because all I can think of is how it all tastes different, smells different, this whole scene tonight, it's unpleasant, it's . . . stupid. When she is done, she looks up at me and smiles, and for the first time I see that she isn't pretty at all, and worse, that she has no teeth. Her face looks like a skull in the lamplight. She slips her dress over her head, reaches over, pulls the door handle, and then climbs over me to get out. I pull on my clothes and see into the front seat as I try to struggle out for some air, promising myself that this is the last time, it has to be, because her skull-face must be some weird kind of warning of death or something. Richard and the fag are doing something in the front, I see, that I know I never wanted to see, and I make it out of the car just in time to stop an unstoppable upward rush from the pit of my stomach.

FOURTEEN

I get up in the morning a little late, nervous. Group session is today. I dress slowly, knowing I don't want to go. I pick up the phone and dial the first four numbers at Kate's, then hang up.

There are other people in the room when I walk in. Kate. And the doctor from the Reynolds Emergency Room; I recognize her at once but don't say anything. How can I? I think. There's also a girl I don't know, looks about my age, pretty.

"Morning, Deed," says Kate, smiling, which makes me feel better.

"Hi!" Carolyn says.

"I'm sorry I'm late. My alarm . . ." I say, sure they know it's a lie.

"Don't worry about it," says Carolyn. "Do you want some coffee?"

"No, thanks, not so early."

"Really? It doesn't do me any good except in the morning."

"I never drink it," the girl says. I look at her, and when my eyes get to hers, hers jump away from mine.

"Good for you," Carolyn says, walking toward her desk. Then: "Deed, this is Jane Weller, a doctor at Reynolds Center; she'll be sitting in for a couple of weeks. And Molly Goldman, another patient."

"Friend," corrects Kate from across the room.

Molly and Jane and I all trade smiles.

"Sorry. Friend." Carolyn is at the coffee machine. "Anyone else for caffeine?"

No one takes her up on it. We begin. First, Jane and Molly give me their phone numbers, and I give them mine. By having the others' phone numbers, all of us will have a support system, so Carolyn says, and it will bind us together. Carolyn asks me to start, and for some reason I no longer feel as nervous. I tell them all directly.

"I tried to kill myself." I turn to Carolyn. "What else?"

"Anything you want. Talk to us."

"I can't do that."

"It's easy, Deed," Kate says. "Try it."

I breathe deep once and look at Jane. Her eyes are on me, red, like she's been crying. She looks nervous. "I'm not sure why I did what I did, but I'm working on it." I smile briefly at Carolyn, then at Kate. "And I feel better, I really do. In the past couple of days, I've figured out some of the reasons why I did what I did. Good reasons— Well, just reasons. I guess we'll see."

Suddenly I know what I want to say, but I become afraid because Jane is here, looking at me, surely recognizing me from yesterday.

"You know, I've seen you before," I say to her.

Jane perks up, surprised out of whatever trance she was in. "Me?"

"Yeah, yesterday, around the corner."

She looks puzzled.

"In the morning," I tell her, "when that little boy was brought in."

She looks away now, her eyes blinking, at the floor, then to Carolyn, then back at the floor.

"—Deed—" from Carolyn.

"I saw you tell the parents he had died," I go on. "Why did he die?"

"—Deed—"

"What?" I say.

"Was that what was wrong yesterday?"

"Part of it," I say, but my eyes are still on Jane. Out of the corners of my eyes, I can see Kate, her face turned toward me, and Molly, her face turned toward Jane. I think for an instant what I'm doing. Is an answer to this why important? Am I being malicious on purpose, because I think that boy should be alive, or is it just a new sensitivity to death? It occurs to me that I don't even know this woman, Jane, and yet I am obviously causing her pain.

"Then I think we can find another topic. Jane's not quite ready to discuss that."

"No, Carolyn," Jane says now. "It's okay." She turns to me. "Deed was there yesterday, I thought I knew him from somewhere. Now I know. The boy died. Do you want to know his name? Patrick Carver. He'd been hit by a car, a drunk driver. One of his lungs was crushed, among other things, and he was in a coma. We thought we might be able to save him, but only with surgery." She stops a moment. "I know what you're thinking. You're thinking, Why didn't you operate, then? The answer is, there were releases to be signed, information to get, and we discovered his parents couldn't afford the operation. No money, no insurance . . ."

"—Jane—" from Carolyn, who could see that it was becoming more difficult for Jane to speak. Her voice had become strained, tight in her throat. We all saw it and heard it. I wanted her to stop, but I didn't dare say another word; besides, I deserved to hear this.

". . . and the policy at Reynolds Center is: No insurance, no treatment. His parents," she says, crying now, "his parents couldn't afford to save him—"

Then Jane jumps up and runs out of the room. Carolyn and Kate follow her, Carolyn motioning with her hand for Molly and me to stay put. I feel like a shit, a real shit, and I cover my face with my hands, trying desperately to keep out the pictures I know are on their way into my eyes. How could I have done this to her, brought up Jane's own painful images like that, without even thinking? Haven't I learned anything at all? For a minute I just sit there, going over it in my head, fending off the faces. Then I remember Molly.

I look at her. She's in a chair near Carolyn's desk, her eyes closed to the scene, to the noise, to it all, breathing deeply.

"What do you think, Molly?"

Startled, she snaps her face in my direction. "Me? I think it's terrible. But I also think there's more to it than that."

"Do you think they're coming back?"

She shrugs, "I don't know," and I think about how Carolyn feels about the phrase, and now there seems even more I don't know. Molly looks at her Swatch, the clear one.

"You have somewhere to go?" I ask.

"No, I'm just hungry, I didn't have breakfast. Hey, you want to have lunch?"

I sit there a second, trying to figure this out. Finally, I decide that not everything has to make sense all the time, and so fuck it, what's done is done, like Kate said about Marian. I write Carolyn a note, and we both sign it, and we leave.

FIFTEEN

Molly and I go to the Jax Brewery for lunch, down on Decatur. To me, the Brewery looks like Beverly Hills, a lot like Beverly Hills, or at least the way Beverly Hills should look: white-white walls, mirrors everywhere, glittery bangles, expensive clothes, and women dressed in awful costumes they call "fashion." If I ever get to Beverly Hills, I'll be disappointed if it doesn't look like the Brewery.

We ride the escalators to three, where there are many booths which have all kinds of Cajun food. The Parasites' dream. There are huge papier-mâché sculptures hanging in the escalator well, for Mardi Gras.

Molly has a yogurt with fruit, and I have a burger. You have to be in the mood for Cajun. We sit in an area sectioned off for eaters, but we move outside to the patio, which overlooks the river, because the seats aren't very comfortable. And besides, the sun is out, the sky is clear, and there's a nice breeze—a beautiful day. We don't talk much, I don't know why. I guess there isn't much to say except things like "Do you have any brothers or sisters?" which I hate, so I don't say anything yet. The whole way down here, all we did was look out the streetcar windows at the scenery along St. Charles, and now all I do is look at her. She is much prettier in the sunlight. Not as tall as I am, fairly curvy and on the thin side, very blond hair with some red in it somewhere, and a terrific smile, though nothing like Kate's. And her hands, they're long and delicate-looking, with clear-polished nails. Much like my mother's.

After lunch I take her down to two to try on hats in some place called Hats in the Belfry. One has a string you pull to make the attached ears flop. Another is a genuine imitation pith helmet. Then we're off to Mrs. Fields', where I buy a small collection of oatmeal-raisins. For a second, only a second, I think of Marian. Molly takes my arm and pulls me across the hall, where she has spotted Steve's Ice Cream. There's no line and she runs in and orders a cup of Oreo with crushed Reese's peanut butter cups mixed in. She takes one taste, then says, "Mmmmmmm, there's nothing like it," like she knows what she's talking about. "Here," and she gives me a taste from her spoon. First reaction: The girl knows her ice cream. I take an oatmeal-raisin from the bag and scoop a hunk of the mixture onto it, then shove it into my mouth. Molly laughs, and I do it again, this time shoving it in her direction.

"With an idea like this, we could open our own shop," she says. Her face lights up like Kate's when she laughs.

Outside, we walk around the neighborhood, around Jackson Square. Today, the artists are out in force, hawking their works to Parasites and natives both. Several of them are into caricatures, but only one looks any good. One water-paints scenes of jamming jazzmen. Many more do pastels of people who are willing to sit and model for an hour in the hot sun, even on this winter day, under the shade of only a small umbrella. The cast-iron fence that surrounds the square is covered with art, hung on hooks and rope. We can barely see into the park on the other side.

The square appears wide open today, a sunny oasis in the longish shadows of the French Quarter, ruffled by the river breeze. Two guys fly a Frisbee, and there's a small stage where a group of musicians fill the air with true Dixie jazz. Pigeons are everywhere, but mostly on the dung-coated statue of Andrew Jackson on his horse, in the center of the lawn. And the magnificent St. Louis Cathedral behind him, tall and pointed in its three spires. From here, you can sometimes see the uppermost parts of the tankers and steamships floating on the Mississippi, only seventy-five yards away, on the other side of the Moonwalk.

Down Decatur a few blocks, near the Central Grocery, the traveling paddle wheel's calliope starts up, making the whole area sound like a parish carnival. As we walk past the grocery, a man and a woman walk out, carrying two halves of a muffelata, and the odors of olives and ham and oils all fill the air. A little ways down, and the smells of the open-air French Market blow our way, the fruits and the vegetables growing hotter, even on this February afternoon.

The whole Quarter—the whole world—seems alive today. The ancient ghosts of the area, of Tennessee Williams and Lillian Hellman, and all their heroes, of the French and Spanish who lived down here, of the servants who lived here after them—all the ghosts must be out today, flitting in and out of the strollers, one by one, spreading whatever it is they spread to make the French Quarter the way it is. It occurs to me that I haven't been down here during the day in ages—I can't even remember the last time.

Where the French Market ends, the Flea Market begins, and then there's Desire, the streetcar, out in the sun, near the Mint. I wonder how many of the Parasites know that Elysian Fields is right here, a walk away.

Above all, today feels as if someone, someone huge and powerful, lifted the Quarter out of Dixieland and dipped it in a vat of romance. At night, these same streets—*rues*—are boiled in a vat of pepper, red and hot. It comes as a surprise to me that during the day it can be so different, so totally different from the way I know the Quarter best, at night. It's a new smell, with new sights and sounds, a new personality, really a new place. Looking around, holding Molly's hand, it seems made of pure romance, like the house in the forest was made of cookies and candy. Even more, today there is no witch.

A couple of left turns bring us deep into the Quarter, into the residential area, past the bebop of jazz clubs and the sexy sweat of Bourbon. All the way down Royal, and the other streets, there are used-book stores, small, ancient hotels, and renovations everywhere. In every block, as we walk, it seems men are painting or hammering or polishing wood or brass. The noises are new, of building, of production, of the future, hanging lightly in the absolute quiet. You can hear the other noises of decadence, of business, of the "other" French Quarter, only if you listen, only if you really want to hear it. It even smells different down this way, almost like the country, much cleaner, with only a hint of booze, from the bars on some of the corners.

Soon enough, Molly and I get up to around the seven or six hundred block of Royal Street, where it all begins, or ends, depending on your direction. Now there are antique shops, T-shirt shops, art galleries. Down Pirate's Alley, dark in the afternoon shade, is the backside of St. Louis Cathedral, and that's where I announce my craving. I grab Molly's hand and pull her through the crowds, across the square, through dozens of pigeons (like the ones in the old black-and-white of my four grandparents in Europe) which seem to leap into the air, all at once, and around the huge statue of Andrew Jackson, to Café du Monde. There's a free table, so we sit. I order hot chocolate and beignets. All Molly wants is water. It all comes quickly, and Molly goes for the powdered sugar and knocks it over. Sugar spews everywhere, and suddenly we are in a cloud of our own. Molly laughs and laughs. She grabs a beignet and wipes up the sugar with it, then stuffs it into my mouth. Then she says, "Come on, let's go," and I drop three ones on the table and she pulls me into the street. We walk back over toward the Brewery, but this time go up and over to the Moonwalk (named, I think, for two reasons: the view of the night sky from here and—and *this* is great—one of our mayors, Moon Landrieu), which for a couple hundred yards lines the water of the muddy Mississippi, and where the sun has conveniently begun to turn the sky pink and orange. In the struggling moonlight, the bubbles of the skylift float like fireflies in a regulation army line.

After dark, we walk back across to Decatur, where a man has set up his huge white telescope. The sky is cloudless, and the stars are abundant. A sign says we can see Saturn, including the rings, for only a buck's "donation." Molly peers in, and her mouth drops open.

"Whoa . . ." she says, stretching the syllable out, which makes it a much stronger reaction to such an impressive sight.

I look in, and sure enough, it's Saturn, rings and all. Impressive, but it looks a little like a card in the eyepiece. I can't be sure, but I think so. This *is* the Quarter at night. Still, I drop two singles into the guy's basket, and we walk up Decatur to Canal, then to Poydras, and over to where the entrance to the World's Fair used to be, where two giant, topless mermaids sat on top of the main gate, their massive breasts tipped with fully erect nipples and their highly visible and shapely asses the targets of a great controversy. Ho-hum.

It is desolate now. Every bit of color gone. Even the spectacular Wonderwall has been torn away. I stand here with Molly and all I can think of is how much fun the Fair was. It was just before I met Marian, and after I met her, and she and I came to the Fair all the time, especially after dark, when there were nightly fireworks over the river around ten-thirty. It was cheaper to get in later in the day, when the exhibits were closed but the rides and things were still open.

The one attraction still left is the skylift across the Mississippi. I take Molly's hand and pay the man four dollars, and we get into a small metal-and-plexy bubble. It lifts us away into the darkness over the river. When we get up high, we can see the city spread beneath us, all lit up like computer chips in the techno-videos on MTV.

"It's gorgeous," she says, and I get a good look at her dark eyes for the first time. The city below, all the twinkling lights, makes her eyes mysterious, beautiful.

"You've never been up here before?"

"No, I was afraid during the Fair."

"You're not afraid now, are you?"

"No." She looks from the view to me. Those eyes.

I look at her closely, and I kiss her softly. She puts her arms around me, and then she is kissing me, too. We hug this way for a long time. I close my eyes, and I think I may never want to let go. I already know Molly means more to me than Marian ever did, but comparing them is silly. Still . . .

It takes only fifteen minutes for the lift to go back and forth one time, and that's with a change of bubbles on the other side, but when I look at my watch again, nearly an hour has passed, and we have not left our holding pattern. The man I paid finally stops our bubble and opens our door when they are closing for the night. I thank him as we leave. He winks.

We ride the streetcar up St. Charles, past Lee Circle, where the General stands high, his arms crossed on his chest, his wide-brimmed hat level on his head, and his eyes turned north, protecting Dixie from another Union invasion. The car stops before Napoleon because there's a parade. Molly and I get out and walk over. There's a nice cool breeze tonight, and I like the feeling of Molly's hand in mine. The crowd presses us together, and eventually I put my arm around her. I hadn't done this before because I'm not terribly good at taking the initiative. Never mind the hour I spent kissing her; an arm around the shoulders is different, and I want to do things right this time. When I put it there, though, it feels above all like it belongs there. Nice.

When we get into the crowd, near an oak tree, I stand behind her, my arms around her waist. The crowd yells to the men on the floats, but we are quiet, just watching the lights and the colors and the madness. For a while, I am lost in the noise and the images and, mostly, the smell of Molly's perfume, which I recognize as Tuxedo, because Becky wears it; it has been my favorite scent since smell one.

Once the parade has gone by, the crowd is gone in minutes. We have not moved from our spot near the tree. The pressing crowd gone, we are still attached. Or is it drawn? Molly turns to face me. Her face is pale in the streetlight, and her eyes sparkle. She's smiling.

"Did you have fun today?"

I want very much for her to say yes, and she says, "It was one of the best days ever. Thank you."

"You're thanking me? But . . ."

"Don't thank me. Just tell me I'll see you again sometime."

I feel her arms tighten on me. I know that I love her. Already, there is no question. Immediately, I am afraid of losing her, yet also afraid of becoming too attached. Mostly, I'm scared to death of feeling this feeling for the first time. For a moment, I think about answering her, then she lays her head on my chest, and I decide I don't need to. But her voice plays over and over in my ears: "Just tell me I'll see you again sometime." I close my eyes to the lights, and open my ears to the sound of the wind in the trees, and hold her tightly.

SIXTEEN

My father and I eat breakfast at the Grill. We used to do it a lot when I was young, just before my mother was killed. Not once since. I think that's because she used to be out on the patio, the cat in her lap, listening to Beethoven and reading the paper when we got home. Now, she won't be there. Funny, I don't think anyone has touched those records in all this time.

We both have an omelette, his with chili, mine with turkey. Coffee for us both, orange juice. And fries.

No mayo.

"You got home late last night," he says.

"Yeah," I say back.

"Have fun?"

"Yeah," I say back. "A lot."

"Who is she?" he asks, looks at me

"How do you know it was a she?" I want to know. I haven't even seen him since he left for the office yesterday.

"Your friend called. Kate," he says.

I say nothing, just look at him. I reach for a fry and he says, "I'm glad, Deed," so my hand never gets there.

"Her name is Molly," I tell him, and his eyes widen a

little, which they haven't done since Mom was alive. When his eyes widen like this it means he has been pleasantly surprised. Molly was his mother's name.

"You met her at . . . ?"

"Carolyn's," I finish for him.

"How is that going?"

"I like it. It's hard to talk sometimes, and I guess there are some problems, but nothing major."

He finishes his omelette and sips his coffee, which is black. I eat most of the fries. "I think it would be a good idea to start having breakfasts here again, like we used to, don't you think?"

I look at him because I'm not sure he has really said that. Breakfast at the Grill was something only he and I shared, and there's never been much of that, and though the talk was always sparse, like today, it meant something. Like today. More than anything, it was the time, and there's been next to none for a too long time. Partly because of Frankie, but also because of the way it always was with us. My eyes on his, I say, "Yes."

There were weekends when I was a boy when we used to go fishing. We'd get up early, before the sun, and drive a long time to the water. Once, we passed a huge canyon, or something that looked like a canyon, and it was filled with billowy clouds and hidden sunlight. From the bridge, it looked like it went on, out, forever, like no matter how far we drove, how close we came, we'd never get to the end.

Fishing was a good time. There was a camp where we stayed, among the oil rigs in the delta, where the Mississippi meets the Gulf of Mexico, owned by a fishing couple; the wife cooked every moment, and her best thing was a tray of baked-in-butter crab claws.

My dad and I were up with the sun every day, and in the skiff for hours, casting into the reeds for redfish. We caught all kinds, though, speckled trout, croakers, catfish. There were times we actually caught a redfish; you could tell because it had a big brown spot on its tail. He called the catfish "pussies" because they were a bitch to get off the line, and sometimes he lost his hook doing it: You have to have a catfish hook to flip them over the line and back into the water. Every once in a while, in the Gulf, Dad'd catch a small shark, and he'd have to shoot it, but not until he beat it over the head with a hammer a few times.

At the reeds there were all sorts of special places to cast: California Point, Hossie's Gulch, like that. Proof that many years and many hopeful fishermen had passed this way. One trip, at California Point, we caught so many reds we had to stop because we ran out of room in the boxes; that day, we could do no wrong. Every time the line hit the water, it came up red. Even for me.

Sometimes we put the fish in baskets, and they'd flip-flop inside for a while, and croakers would belch, until they died. Sometimes when I was bored I'd press their dead eyes around in their sockets. The eyes were like glass, except they were mushy, slimy, like their skin. Once, I ran my hand the length of a fish in the wrong direction and cut my hand on its scales.

Other times I imagined we were being chased by an enormous shark. Then I saw *Jaws* and stopped.

Whenever I caught a red, that was a great fishing moment. What I loved was fighting them, doing it all myself. Usually, Dad would put his pole aside and watch until I had the fish close to the skiff, then he would take the net and scoop the fish into the boat. He always took out the hook.

The tackle box we used was filled with fishing stuff, each thing in its own little space. There were many, many lures, with whiskers, or eyes, and with little hooks coming out, and worms with little hooks. All kinds of things to fool the fish with. I don't know if any worked.

Showers at the camp were an experience, because there was no hot water. For that matter, there was no *running* water. We'd have to go down to the two-by-four floor near the water, near the pier, and hose each other up and down with icy water. And taking a shit was fun, too, because there was no pressure to fill the toilet tank back up, so before you went, you had to go down to the water and fill up the bathroom bucket and pour it into the tank.

And Dad always pissed over the side of the skiff.

The last time we went, we were caught by a storm. We were in Hossie's Gulch, doing pretty well for so late in the morning, when the blue sky disappeared behind a black cloud—black. That was when the temperature dropped and the wind blew up out of nowhere, shooting pinpricks of rain into us. Dad couldn't get the motor started, he just pulled at the cord, and the skiff was filling with water, and I was trying to splash it over the side. When he finally got the thing started, it was raining so hard we couldn't see where we were going, and we ran onto the shells (the water was only a few inches deep). So we paddled out and rowed back to camp.

For so long—maybe too long—I'd forgotten the fishing, put it out of my mind, really. But when my father comes into my room later, after lunch, and starts talking, the fishing creeps back into me like a familiar smell. I hear his words, listening to wanted sentences and remembering wanted images, and I remain silent.

"Remember when we went to the Grill when you were a boy, before your mother died? And we used to order just what we had today? And we'd go home, and she'd be on the patio, in one of the big chairs, curled up with the paper, with her music on? Sometimes I think about how it used to be, and how it is now, and I don't know how to change it. I used to think I could, but I don't know anymore. I just know when I saw you in that bathroom, on the floor, with all that blood, I almost died. All I could think about was how you used to come in there to watch me shave in the mornings, before school, and how your mother would get angry and yell from downstairs that I'd be late for work and you and Becky would miss your bus. And when I picked you up I saw the blade on the floor, under you, and I began to shake because it was one of my old blades. It was like someone had slapped me on the face. Then, when you were in that bed, with the bandages on your wrist, all I could think of was the word 'live.' It was almost like a command, for a while. *Live, dammit, live.* Then I realized that I couldn't command you to live. So then all I wanted was for you to *want* to live. I wanted it more than anything. There was a moment when you opened your eyes, when Becky had come, and I wanted so much for your mother to be there with me, or even instead of me, because I knew *her* face would have made you want to live. Not mine. I used to lie in bed at night, alone, and smell her old perfumes. If I closed my eyes, I could almost feel her next to me. I haven't done that in years. You must do things like that, too. I know how close you were to her, much closer than you were to me. I know now that was my fault, trying to make you something you didn't want to be. At the beginning, after she died, I know we all stayed together to get over her death, and then suddenly it stopped. We stopped handling it together, as a family. I know I still need to, sometimes. And I wish we could all start to handle it again, together. It would help. There are so many things I've wanted to say to you, for so long, that now I'm afraid there are just too many. Things have been coming down on you lately, I know, especially with Jason and Chip. Losing them is something I can't even understand, except if I go back and remember losing *my* best friend, your mother. I know losing them must be harder on you, because she's already gone. I wish you would, or could, come to me for the comfort and understanding she'd give you. One day, I hope you will. Walt . . . Deed, I've known for a long time what the problem was with us. We've been at odds, sort of, since the beginning, on nearly every subject, from sports to sex. And I've known I was the one who needed to talk first, especially because of Frankie, but I didn't know how to do it. I . . . still don't. But I feel like I have to try. I don't want to lose you, like I did your mother. I feel like there *has* to be a way for us to put Frankie behind us, forever. I have an idea you've put her behind you, and she's long gone as far as I'm concerned—but she's still between us. It has to stop. All this time, I never thought about what it meant to you, I never thought it was very important, I guess. I mean, I'm a man, you're my son, and what happened with Frankie was something that shouldn't have ever happened. But it did. It couldn't be stopped, not then. No one could have known what would happen, no one could have stopped it. I couldn't. I never thought of it the way you did, like I was cheating on you. It never occurred to me, and I know *that's* part of the problem. For me, it was just a good time, a good time which I might have shared with you. That's the truth about it. If I had thought I was hurting you, I never would have done it. I wouldn't have allowed it. For me, it meant something else, something harmless. Frankie pushed herself into our family through you, and I know that must have hurt you, seeing what she did, what she and I did. I guess we'll never know what she was after. I don't think she got it, whatever it was. I never knew how important she was to you, and I never dreamed I could hurt you so much by letting her do what she did to me, to all of us. I can't make excuses, I can't tell you she hypnotized me or anything, because she didn't. I knew what I was doing, and it's something I'll have to live with forever. I knew in the end how important it was, how significant it was to us all, but by then it was too late. What could I have said? There was so much anger in the way. I've been thinking about it all again, since you were in the hospital. And I can't stop believing that what you did was my fault. What I did with Frankie was a slap in the face to you. We did it to you. I didn't see it then, but I see it now . . ."

I remember he used to take me to the Saints football games at Tulane Stadium when I was a kid. We sat way up in the stadium in the middle of the field. We would eat peanuts and cotton candy, and the popcorn came in cardboard megaphones you could yell through after the food was gone. I used to take his binoculars—"binocs," he used to call them—and watch the people watching the game. Usually that was the best part. The only other time it was fun, and this didn't happen a lot, was when the Saints won, and my dad would take me in his arms and throw me up in the air again and again, and we would laugh.

". . . We always see better in retrospect. That's one of our flaws. I hope it's not too late. Having an affair was something I only associated with being married. I never thought about it, about the family. It never occurred to me that what I did was the same thing as having an affair. I betrayed you, Deed. I betrayed a trust we had in each other. I know that. What I did was just the same as if I had had an affair when your mother was alive. I know that now. And I know it meant more to you than I thought it did, than it meant to me. I know it hurt you in a way you should never have been hurt, not only the affair, but also the lies. I know that. I know. Believe me. I also know that nothing means more to me than you and Becky. Nothing ever meant more to me than this family. You have to believe that, Deed. The way we raised you, we were never parents and kids; we were all good friends, weren't we? Best friends. Your mother and I wanted to raise you not to be afraid, to believe in what was right and good. Even though it looked like I lost track of what was good, if I *did* lose it, I've found it again, and I still want that for both of you. I want to find a way to get us all back to being best friends. Nothing I say to you now can change the past, and I can only explain it a certain way, in the most honest way I can. There's only one truth to it all, and you know the facts. We can't change them, even though I wish we could. I wish we could go all the way back and start over, from when you were born. I'd do things right. I would. I'd make sure you were happy. I'd earn the right to be your best friend. But then we wouldn't be here now. We'd be different people. I don't know if we'd even be better, or as good, or any happier. I do know that I'm sorry, Deed, sorry for everything. For expecting you to understand things you couldn't, for putting you through things you should never have seen, for lying to you the way I did, for trying to make you just like me, the way my father made me just like him. If there's anything I can say or do to get us back on track again, I'll do it. I will. I want to make things right again, the way they were. None of us will ever forget Frankie, and you may never even forgive me, but we will go on, Deed. We have to. There *is* a future, for all of us. And we can't let the past screw it up for us. It wasn't worth it, it wasn't worth it. For now, all I want is for you to know I'm sorry, and to think about it a while. I never say it anymore, because I'm not sure you want to hear it, or if it will mean anything to you, but, Deed, I love you. I always will. I always did."

"I've been thinking," I tell Carolyn. We are walking this afternoon, the sun is slowly setting and it's not cold, though there's a nice breeze.

Carolyn seems preoccupied, though, and I can't get her to tell me what it is. She's anxious to be outside when I arrive. I guess the windows in her office aren't enough today. "About what?" she asks.

"Wordsworth."

We keep walking, blocks and blocks along St. Charles Avenue in the shade, toward the park. Every few minutes, a streetcar dings behind us and we move over to the other track. Once, there are two, one going each way, and we are caught between; the two of them create a spontaneous vacuum, and I feel pulled, yet repelled, by both. Oddly, it's a sensation I deplore and adore, at once.

"Jason wasn't a happy guy," I say. "There was too much he had problems with. He wasn't popular, he didn't have any friends except me. He was a straitlaced kid."

"Why were you his friend?"

"We met in grade school. He was popular then, really popular. He was great in gym, he could run faster than anybody else. I guess I looked up to him, secretly, which was kind of funny, too, because he was shorter than I was, looked younger. Back then I wasn't the athlete I am now—"

Carolyn chuckles.

"—and I think he felt sorry for me. I don't know. I just know we were never enemies, really, like I was with the other guys. Jason never cared that I was different. He took an interest in me. After eighth grade, we both left Newman to go to Franklin. By then, we had the same problem: No one liked us. He was on top of everything in May, at the end of seventh grade, but by the time September came, he was out. That was the beginning of eighth grade. Now that I think of it, I don't know if we ever found out why the guys decided to stop liking him. We never talked about it. Then we became best friends."

"Did it get better at Franklin?"

"No, not really. We had a few pals, not many, no one popular. We were all sort of a ragtag group. The leftovers, maybe. Yeah. There were the ones who wore those little black slippers all the time, the girls, and the ones who ate health food and were vegetarians because it was the thing *not* to do, and the science fiction addicts, but by then the *Star Wars* movies had turned *everybody* into science fiction addicts. And us, I don't know, the misfits. All Jason ever wanted was to get back where he'd been before, when we were at Newman. He wanted to be popular again."

"He never got there, did he," she says as a statement, really, not a question.

"Uh-uh," I say. "I guess he . . . I guess he died trying."

We walk on. In a few minutes, we reach the next intersection.

"I feel like now I have to get us *both* back to where he was before. You know?"

She says nothing.

"Is that wrong?"

"No," Carolyn says. "It's not wrong, but, Deed, you can't live for Jason. Do you know what I mean? Live for *you,* not him. Don't fall into the trap he did. He wouldn't want that, would he?"

There's a red light at Jefferson, only a block from the Octavia, where Kate lives, and about a mile from the park.

"You think we ought to turn back?"

"Okay," I say.

"How's the situation with Marian?"

"I don't know. No change. I haven't really thought about it. I've been too busy with other things."

"Like Molly, maybe?"

I nod a couple of times.

"We saw you leave with her yesterday," she tells me.

"We went to Jax for lunch."

"You had fun?"

"The best."

"That's what she said," and I look at her sideways. She reaches into her pocket and pulls out a pack of Camels. She takes one out to suck. Then she glances at me, sees my surprise. "She called me early this morning."

I smile, remembering. Eventually, we walk right past the oak tree Molly and I stood under last night.

"There's a lot you don't know about her, Deed," Carolyn says, "and I'm not the one to tell you any of it. Maybe she will, in time. She needs someone like you, someone to trust. The two of you meeting is a great part of what makes my program work as well as it does."

"Yeah, I thought so. It works that way with Kate, too," I say. "Molly seems fragile, yet strong in some ways. Maybe a little vulnerable."

"Very vulnerable. You can do a lot of harm. I know it seems like a lot to ask, but before you two get really hooked on each other, I'd like you to do some thinking about it. I don't know if she could take a great disappointment in her life right now. Do you know what I mean? I think if anything happened to her, you'd be hurt, too. So please, please be careful with her."

"Look, I can promise you that. Yesterday was unbelievable. It really was, for us both. There's some sort of connection there. And I've already thought about what I feel, and all that."

"Good. Just . . . be careful, Deed. As I said, there are things you don't know. I don't want to say 'dangerous,' because I don't want to scare you. But I want you to be—there isn't another word—be careful. Use your head.

She's not like, I don't know, other girls. I know that sounds silly. Will you take my word for it?"

We keep walking and I turn it over in my head. When we finally get back to her office, her receptionist tells her she has another hour until Jane Weller's appointment. "Would you like to stay a while longer?"

"Sure. Is Jane okay? I meant to ask you. I'm sorry about yesterday."

"She's okay. Kate and I spoke to her for a while. That little boy's death really shook her up. That's why she wants to sit in with the group for a while. She's been fighting that policy the whole time she's been at Reynolds."

"I didn't know."

"She knows that. She doesn't blame you. It just wasn't the best time to talk about it. It was too soon. And she never dreamed anyone would bring it up before she was ready."

I tell her that when I saw her tell the boy's parents that he was dead, all I could think of was my mother, and how some doctor or policeman had to tell my dad. I was angry and frustrated, I tell her, and it just came out the wrong way.

In her office now, I begin to pace the room. I keep my eye on the colored sculpture. "Who did you say made that?"

"Agam."

"Yeah," remembering.

"I bought it in Israel a few years ago. I knew it would be perfect there. The changes fascinate me."

"Me, too. It's exciting." I look at it closely now. "It's almost like a person. It's like if we walk from here"—I walk it—"to here, it looks different. Almost the way a person changes sometimes, right before your eyes. With time . . ."

She interrupts: "Or perspective."

"Yeah," I say, and look at her. "Exactly, perspective."

"Tell me what you see in that one," she says, pointing to the one with the girl in a wheat field, with the barn and the house in the distance.

"That one?" I look at it, closer now. "It's almost the same thing," I say. "Perspective. I mean, you *know* she's thinking about what happened in that barn, years ago, and she's wondering if things are still the same, or if they've changed." I think a moment, then say, "If this were a photograph, I bet she would jump up in the next second and run to the barn or that house and find whoever she's thinking about."

"She can't do that, she can't run," Carolyn says. "She's crippled, Deed. She can barely walk. The crutch she uses is in front of her, hidden by her body."

I don't say anything, I just stand there looking at the girl.

I hear Carolyn's voice: "Nothing else will change for her. She lives every day with the memory of what happened to her."

My eyes don't leave the girl, but I say, "What happened to her?" All at once, I feel sad, and for a moment I remember the pictures from my mom's trunk in the attic.

"I don't know," she says, and I turn around to look at her face.

For a moment, we stand there facing each other, sending messages of sadness and understanding back and forth. Then she says, "Does it make getting back into living any easier?"

"I think so," I say. "So far, it does. How about for you?"

"For me?"

"Yeah."

"What do you mean?"

"Your mother," I say.

She looks at me now, then stands and walks to the large window. Below is St. Charles, and a clanking streetcar. She glances over at the photograph of the young woman, the black-and-white, it must be her mother.

"It's easier. Most of the time. I never knew my mother, she died giving birth to me. That's been a tough one to deal with. I grew up on my father's knee. It was pretty bumpy, but it was okay. I didn't miss having a mother because I didn't know what having a mother was like."

"I wanted to ask you about that."

"What?" She looks over at me again.

"About missing her. Did you?"

"I missed her, I guess, a little. But not really. I missed *knowing* her, you know? I missed having the chance to know her, I missed the answers to all my questions about her, like exactly what her hands looked like, or the color of her hair, or how she looked when she laughed."

"My mother was killed when I was eight. So I had eight years with her. I don't remember most of it, not really, just from pictures. When she was gone, it was so painful. Sometimes I miss her so much, and I can just hear her voice, or her laugh."

"That's the difference. You can hear it. I can't. I never did. You miss having her with you, and you might even wish sometimes that you never knew her, so it wouldn't hurt so much now. But I would give anything to have had my mother, even only for eight years. Or for one year. Or a day."

Carolyn looks away from me, out the window. She puts her hands up, flat on the glass. "The worst times for me were other kids' birthday parties, when I was little. All my friends had their mothers there . . . I don't know. She's why I'm here now."

"What does that mean?"

She takes another drag on the cigarette, the same one,

still dry. "I became a shrink because I needed to be in constant touch with other people. I need to help them, and to be needed by them. To mother them, maybe. But it doesn't work as much as I'd like. I don't mother you, at least I hope I don't. But I do care about you," she says, looking out the window still, "all of you. And I need you as much as you need me . . ."

I go over to her and stand nearby.

"Did you ever . . ." I say, then stop.

"What?"

"It's not important."

"Tell me."

"Who started the group?"

"I did."

"Why?"

"To help people recover, to come back over the wall, I guess. Like Kate says, to help them get back into living. To give them a real place to come, to belong, to be loved, and listened to."

She is quiet for a while. I can hear the sounds of her breathing, and of the street five floors below. For just a moment, her body shudders, as if she is holding back the torrent of her pent-up emotion. Then it's passed, and she says, "I know what you wanted to say." She stops. Then: "It was a long, long time ago."

I am still beside her, and for a minute we just stand there, as if we're listening to each other breathe. I look over the office once more. The photograph of her mother, the Wordsworth, the girl in the field, the Agam. I have stood here before to see a pattern in the Agam. I glance back at the photograph, and in the dark background I can see the colors of the Agam, reflected backwards, and a completely new pattern is born.

SEVENTEEN

In the morning I go to the Metronome to ask Guy if I can start working again, part-time. He says I can. I stay during the day because he needs someone to price, log, and rack several cartons of albums. Sometime after lunch, someone puts a Phil Collins album on the stereo; not the latest one, but the one with "In the Air Tonight" on it. During the song, Marian appears in the back, where I am putting jazz albums away, as if on cue, and it all comes together suddenly.

"Hi, Deed," she says.

When I look up, I catch the video on the silent MTV; it's a Twisted Sister piece of garbage, which naturally doesn't quite fit with what's coming out of the speakers, or anything else. I say hi, trying to sound like I'm glad she's here.

"How've you been?"

"Good, real good. How are you?"

"Fine, I guess," she says. "I don't know." I try not to look at her. I do not stop the work, partly because Guy wouldn't like it, but mostly because I need to concentrate on something, anything, other than Marian and her pleading tone. I forgot how unattractive it was. "Lonely." Figures, and not too surprising.

Now I have to look up at her. "I'm sorry."

"So am I. I didn't want to say that," she says. She isn't looking at me, but at the floor. "Look, I just came in to look, I didn't know you'd be here."

"I just came back today," I say. "Part-time."

"That's good, Deed." She hears the song for the first time then, or makes as if she does. "Your song," she says, knowing that it isn't my song at all, but was ours, once.

"Yeah. Haven't heard it in a while. So what are you looking for?"

"Nothing. Nothing. I'm just . . . looking." She glances around the store at the wall displays, then turns to look at me again. I have already gone back to the bins. "Bye, Deed, it was good to see you." She turns and walks away, and I say, "You, too," though I think she must know I don't mean it.

Around five a guy from Newman walks in, right past me. He grabs the new Heads and comes back over to the register, where Guy has put me as a sub for the late-afternoon shift. Cliff looks up, and I see his eyes recognize me, trying to quickly place my present face with its younger version from his past, and I'm looking right at him, one of the worst little pricks in the school, years ago. And probably still.

He says, "Walt Smith, right?"

"It's Deed now," I say, surprised that he remembered my name.

"Oh. How have you been?"

"Okay, and you?" I say, and I can't believe I'm standing here talking to him, just like before never was. I always thought, always *knew,* none of them would grow up and see the light. But here he is, talking to me of his own free will, acting like we're old pals. I don't know what to think, so I don't. For now, I figure, just go along with it, and figure it out later, when it won't matter so much. Which leads to: Why does it matter so goddamn much right now?

He says he's okay. "You went to Franklin, right?"

"Yeah, I really liked it. It's a great place."

"That's what I hear. What are you doing now?"

"Nothing. I decided to . . . put off college for a little while," I say.

"I thought about that. But I'm at Tulane. My folks did some pushing."

"Uh-huh," I say. I wonder if he knows how lucky he is to have both alive and pushing. Maybe, I think, he does. He seems capable of that, now.

Someone comes up behind him, and so I punch Cliff's album up with an employee's discount, on impulse. I hand him his bag, and he says, "Thanks, Deed. Maybe I'll see you 'round." He puts his hand out, and before I know what I'm doing, I've taken it and squeezed hard, like I was taught to do.

"Yeah," I say, "it was good to see you," and he smiles, and I think I mean it. As he walks through the double swinging doors to the sun, I suddenly feel a step further on the bridge from childhood to the other side.

Kate and I have dinner at a Chinese place on Maple. I have beef with broccoli and she has something called Foo Soo.

"Tell me about Molly," Kate says, getting the hang of her chopsticks.

"She's a bitch," I say, and Kate's smile dies fast. But her eyes hold mine, and before long I have to laugh, though I am able to keep it to just a smile. Seeing this, Kate laughs out loud.

"You bastard!" she says, and the table next to ours quiets and all of them look over at us, and it must look strange, an eighteen-year-old boy with someone who must be his grandmother, and they're calling each other names.

Using my fork, I take a few strips of beef, then a couple of broccoli trees, and when I look up, Kate is still looking at me, her sticks down, her hands folded. I smile at her briefly, then stuff the trees into my mouth. Then she says softly, "If you don't start talking in the next ten seconds, I'm going to take this chopstick and plunge it into your arm."

"Uh-huh," I say. "Don't you love this place?" Then I smile, looking around a bit. I slowly reach across the table and lift a stick from her plate, and hand it to her.

"How old did you say you were, Deed?"

"Eighteen, right?" I ask.

"You *do* want to make it to nineteen, don't you?" she says, toying with the stick the same way your average mad scientist fondles a scalpel. So sinister.

"You can come up with something better than that," I say. "That's one of the oldest jokes in the book."

"So am I," she says.

I begin to laugh, then Kate begins to laugh, leaning her chair back to give herself room. The table next door quiets again, and they all look over.

Then I tell her, "Molly is wonderful. I'm crazy about her."

"I thought so. That makes me very happy. See how easy that was? Besides," she says, "I spoke to her this morning."

"I figured as much. What does she say about me?"

Kate lifts a mouthful onto her sticks, says, "She says you're a bastard," and stuffs the Foo Soo into her mouth.

"You bitch!" I say, and the table next door leaves.

I ride the streetcar with Kate back to her apartment in the Octavia. She asks me to join her for a little while, inside.

She fixes a pot of tea, "Twining's English Breakfast," she says. Her place is small, but very much like Kate herself—well kept, beautifully decorated, and filled to the rafters with a lifetime of memories.

We sit in the living room, Kate on a love seat, me on a chair nearby. She pours the tea, and steam jumps in curls from the cups.

"You asked me why I tried to drown myself, remember?"

I don't say anything, but I look up at her.

"I think I'm ready to tell you now."

I just look.

"When I turned eighty-three, do you know how many people called me to say 'Happy birthday'? Five. My daughter and her husband, and their kids. By nine A.M. I had heard from all the people in the world who knew it was my birthday. I spent the whole day alone, and I became angry no one had called. I promised myself I would let everyone know how upset I was. What I had forgotten was that there wasn't anyone else. I had forgotten, that day, that all my friends in the world were dead."

I don't say anything. I put my teacup down.

"It's a horrible thing to be the last one. You spend your whole life with people, you grow old together, you know all their secrets and they know yours, all the stories back and forth, everything. And then they're gone. And there are no more stories, no more secrets, no more evenings playing bridge, or canasta, or parties. Nothing. Just a lot of stupid novels." Her lips tremble into a slight smile.

I notice only that I blink.

"That was when it started, after dinner, when I began to think about what my life meant to me. I thought about my best friends, how we had been so young and alive years ago, how we had gone into the world babies and done great things before we were over. Not important things, not for all of us anyway, but things that stay with you. Like helping with aid for the men fighting in Europe. Working. The PTA. Like raising a family to be wise, healthy, and brave. Maybe you're too young . . . But I didn't like remembering it all. I hated it. It felt dead to me, all of it, and that was the worst part . . ."

As I watch, she begins to cry, and her face tightens, tears tracing snail's track lines on her cheeks.

"I could almost smell death all around me, right here in this room. I thought, These are the memories I will always have, until I die, what's left of my life, of our lives together, and they're making me sad. I got up and pulled out the yearbooks, and I looked at all those pictures. I read about what we did, what clubs we were in, what we liked to do on weekends, our favorite quotes. I had forgotten most of it. I laughed a few times, and I felt a little better, but not nearly enough. I finally went to sleep, late. I tried to see their faces in the dark. You have to understand, these are the people I spent my life with, they *were* my life. They still are. Yet I couldn't find their faces in the dark. They didn't come. All I could see was their lives. Their children and their grandchildren. The places they had worked, the honors they had received. All together. Everything but those faces. It was frightening not to be able to see them as I knew them. As people, the best people I knew. My friends, my family. I couldn't sleep. I turned on my light and started reading the paper, and there was an article in the second section about total eclipses. There had been one that day, I think. I had to put the paper down. Those words, 'total eclipse,' struck me. Suddenly I knew why I couldn't find the faces. It was because they were blocked by all the things that made their lives. Between me and the faces of my friends, there were lifetimes of memory, of achievements. What I saw was that when we are alive, life is like a sun. We do things, we feel things, we're even warm. We're part of everything. But all that's left after we die is what we did, our achievements, our past. When we look back, the life itself blocks out so much, like the moon in front of the sun, and we can't see the face. Just the circle of rays, the energy shooting out into space, just memories we have of them, how they were part of our lives, how they made us warm. In a way, we see their lives in eclipse—the expended energy, not the sun, not *them.* That was when I knew I didn't want to be here to see only the memories."

I am still looking at her. I haven't looked away the whole time. She looks down at her cup and pours more tea into it. She asks me if I want more, and I look down at my cup, which is still nearly full, and I drink it all, cold. I don't want any more, I tell her, no more.

EIGHTEEN

As I walk from the waiting room to Carolyn's office, I hear her phone ringing. As I open the door, she waves me in and answers it, on the third ring.

"Hello?"

Then: "Hi, Jane."

Then: "Are you crying?"

Then: "Okay, slow down, slow down."

I take my usual seat near the desk. I can't quite get the conversation from only this end, so I stop listening. But I do hear Carolyn tell Jane to come in, anytime. After about ten more minutes, she hangs up.

She removes a cigarette from her purse, sucks on it dry once, then takes out a lighter. She sucks the flame up into the front end and takes a long, long drag, then lets the smoke lazily float out of her mouth. Her eyes squint with mine, unaccustomed to the sensation. She looks through the fog at me. "Jane just resigned. She quit Reynolds."

I don't ask why. I know why.

"I met with the Board again this morning, early, and we're in trouble." She lights up a second time. "I can't think of anything to do, I've been so rattled about it."

"That sounds like Kate."

"I guess it rubs off," she says, taking another drag. "They say the program is useless, that I'm only seeing four patients, so what good does it do? They don't see the value in understanding *why*. Why is it so impossible for those morons to see it?"

"Can't you tell them?"

"I've been telling them for months. They don't listen. They're determined to shove this program out of the hospital and me off the Board. Jane had it no better, believe me. She's been bucking to change that insurance/treatment policy, remember? And they've been trying to push her out for a long time. Looks like they got what they wanted there."

Jane walks in about twenty minutes later. Her face is red, her eyes puffy. She looks much different from her usual groomed, very yuppied self. She's wearing her white topcoat, from the hospital. "Reynolds Center" is sewn onto it, above her left breast. She's holding her stethoscope in one hand, her purse in the other. She looks at me and I want to say I'm sorry, but then she looks away and my chance is gone. She tosses her stethoscope onto the chair that matches mine, then fishes in her purse for something. When she finds it, she drops it on the desk in front of Carolyn.

"What is it?" Carolyn asks.

Moving her purse, Jane sits. "Lynn."

Carolyn looks at it, then at Jane. "You found it."

"In my office, right after I spoke to you. It's amazing to see what can accumulate in an office. You ought to clean yours out one day."

Carolyn smiles briefly, then looks at me. "Deed, you should probably know what's going on. Is that all right with you?" She looks at Jane.

"Sure, I don't see why not."

"Deed, there was someone else in the group, before you. Her name was Lynn Waters."

Was?

"She totaled her car last year, but she didn't quite do the damage to herself that she wanted to. Her doctor sent her here. We worked with her for weeks. She was very depressed."

"I met her when they brought her into Emergency. I quickly saw that she was smart, popular, attractive," Jane says. "She was what every girl wants to be. But it wasn't enough. Not even close. She was very unhappy. She couldn't find any good in herself. She saw good all around her, but she was blind to her own beauty. Her own goodness."

"When she was sent here, she was pretty badly damaged. She had her bruises, and a crutch, and a temporary eye patch over one eye," says Carolyn, and she looks momentarily at Jane. "There were days, though, when she seemed fine, when none of that mattered. On those days, you could swear she was the happiest girl in the world. And yet, she was miserable the next day. For a long time, I was baffled."

Carolyn stops. They both look at me. All I can think of is my desire to be hit by that truck. The feeling of it. This girl had done it—and lived. But why?

"Then we discovered who her parents were," Jane says. "Very wealthy, but they had a worthless marriage. They ignored her and fought constantly. They were caught up in their own lives, which were almost totally separate from Lynn's, and from each other's. Her father was the worst of the two. He was known for his affairs, and from what Lynn told us, it was a different girl every week or so, most not much older than Lynn. He used to tell her about them. She used to tell me there were days when all she could think of was how she just wanted to tell her mother everything. But she knew that would destroy her."

"Talk about guilt," I say.

"She was absolutely torn by it. Either cover for her father or hurt her mother—that was her choice."

"Wow."

Carolyn lights up for the third time. "And then she met someone," she says, smoke pouring from her mouth, "a guy, we never knew his name. She said she met him at school—"

"What school?"

"Newman. She met him and they started going out. She spent all her time with him. By now, her bandages were off, and she'd started walking."

"She was beautiful again," Jane says.

"Gorgeous," Carolyn adds. "She would come here once, twice a week, most days on top of the world, and a few days down. It was never as bad as it was before the guy, but she was still upset about something."

"And that was about the time she and I became friendly," Jane says. "I'd kept in touch over the weeks after her accident, and little by little, she began to trust me. We took a vacation together at their house in Antigua, for three weeks. It was fantastic. For someone so young, she was terribly sophisticated, so concerned about the future, and where she would fit in. She wanted to be productive, successful. She said the guy talked about marriage, which made her happy." Jane reaches for the pack of cigarettes on the desk. "May I?" She lights one, takes a few smoky drags, blows the smoke out hard, off to the side.

"Then one morning, about a week after Antigua, she was dead. It was in the papers, just like that. They said she jumped out of a window and broke her neck." Jane's voice grows thick.

Carolyn mashes out her cigarette, as if to take revenge on it for Lynn's death. She stares at it while she kills it. "It was very hard. Lynn's parents were out of town, and we were asked to identify the body."

"They called and asked me to go over to the house," Jane continues, "so I went, and there was a note for me. It said, 'Play the tape. That's all. Play it.' The tape was in the stereo in her room. The power was on, and the tape was at the end. Everyone thought it was a note from her, a recorded suicide note or something. Someone rewound it and played it while I was there. It was from her boyfriend, whoever he was. I guess, thinking about it now, it was a suicide note, after all. Just not the kind you hear about. It was a message from the guy, telling her he wanted to break up even though he still loved her. He said he felt, uh, trapped. Anyway, after they played it, I left, and I didn't hear any more about it for a long time. About four months later, I got a package in the mail. Lynn's father had sent me the tape, with the note."

"That's it?" I ask, pointing to the tape on the desk.

"Yeah." Jane picks it up. "It's been in my desk since then, in the same envelope. I'd almost been able to put it out of my mind, until this morning." She looks at Carolyn. "I'd like you to keep it now. I can't just throw it away, but I can't keep it." Abruptly, Jane hands it to Carolyn and looks away, toward the window.

Carolyn weighs it in her hand, then stands up and walks it over to the other side of the room. She drops it into the deck there, pushes PLAY. At first, there's just a hiss, then the sound of someone moving, sitting in a squeaky chair. And then his voice.

NINETEEN

I take Molly to Audubon Park after lunch, and we sit on one of the concrete benches facing St. Charles. For a long time she is quiet. Her dress is light, sheer, and it billows in the breeze. It's a warm day and there are many people around, everywhere, students from Tulane, skaters, joggers in the park and on the avenue. Though it is still "winter" here, I could swear I smell sweet magnolia blossoms on the trees around us. My grandmother would sit here and say, "How de-voon," or something like that; she is very chic. There's a woman with a Newfoundland, a huge one, on the grass. And cyclists everywhere.

"They fight most of the time," Molly says suddenly. I ask who. "My folks. When I come in after school, they're always at each other. I haven't seen my father in weeks, but I hear his voice every day. I walk in the house and he's there, in the bedroom with my mom, and he's drunk, and she's crying, and they're fighting. Mostly I just take an apple from the bowl and go upstairs to my room." She stops, looks around, at the streetcar rolling by. "The stairs at home creak. When I go up, I'm very careful about the stairs. Sometimes I know I'm going to hit it, and I pray so hard that I won't. I know if I hit it then he'll come out of the bedroom and start on me. And I didn't want bruises that night, so I prayed he'd stay in there with her. I heard him get louder, and I thought he knew I was home. I was almost at the top of the stairs. His voice was harsh, he was accusing her of something insignificant, as usual. I really didn't know if it was my mother in there or not. The door was closed. I wished she wasn't in there, that he was screaming at someone else, but I knew she was. She always was. I just went into my room and locked the door. I closed my blinds and lay down on the bed in the dark, and I put my Walkman on and turned it up to ten."

She stops again, it looks like to breathe. Her blond-red hair is caught up in the warm inhale-exhale of the afternoon, and it waves in wispy pieces, everywhere except where sweat has glued it to her skin. I wonder what she is talking about, and why. Why now? It seems like whatever it is, it happened sometime before, before yesterday, before.

"Around seven I got dressed in the dark. I tried to make as little noise as I could. The yelling had stopped. Linda's Sweet Sixteen was that night. Linda's mom and my mom were best friends, so Linda invited me even though I was only thirteen. When I got outside I took off my shoes. Linda's house was only a few houses down, and I used to like to walk in the grass in my bare feet. There was a lot of food there, on great big tables, and so many people. There was a guy from Linda's class who I knew from the halls, at the biggest table. He was looking at all the food, and I walked up to him and said hi. He said hi to me, and said he recognized me from school. I took a plate, and I caught him looking at me. He looked like a movie star, especially when he smiled. He told me to come with him when he went over to the bar. He got two white wines. He gave me one, and we found a place to sit. He asked me about things, but I didn't say too much. I was a little nervous. Then he asked me if I wanted to go somewhere to be alone. He said I looked sad, and we could talk if I wanted. So we went up to Linda's parents' bedroom, and he closed the door, and we sat on the bed. He said, 'Let me rub your shoulders,' and I let him. He began to kiss them, and then he turned me around and kissed me on my mouth for a long time, like we were grown-ups. No one ever kissed me before. I was wearing a halter, and he put his hands on my stomach. I was afraid, but his hands were warm, so it wasn't so bad. He started to push his hand under it, and I was really scared, but he said it was all right. He told me how soft I was, and that I was beautiful. Then he got up and I thought he was leaving, but he locked the door and came back and started taking off his clothes. I didn't move, I couldn't, so I just watched him. I'd never seen anyone's body before, not even my dad's, ever. He was tall, with muscles, and he had blond hair and blue eyes, and the straightest white teeth. When he was done, he began to take my clothes off me. I didn't even feel it. He kissed me some more, and I felt his hands all over me. He pushed me back on the bed, and he put his fingers inside me. He pushed my legs apart and climbed on top of me. 'Relax,' he said. And I thought, nothing. And then he did it to me, and I cried while he kissed me. A couple minutes later it was over, and he put his clothes back on and left me there, in the dark."

I don't take my eyes off her. She is crying, a crumpled piece of paper in her fist. Another streetcar rattles by. Her cottony dress is stuck by the wetness of the winter's heat to her legs, to her back and chest. She takes a deep breath and begins again.

"About a month after that, I began to get sick in the mornings, right before school. But I didn't tell Mom, I didn't tell anybody. One day after school, I came home and it was just like always, and there was cleaning on the kitchen table. Dresses and shirts. I stood there and stared at the clothes, and I took a hanger from one of the shirts and went up to my room and unwound it and went into the bathroom and turned on the hot water all the way. I took off my clothes and put my hand under the water, and it burned, and I thought, This is how I'll remember this, from the burns. I put the hanger in the water and it got hot, and then I put it inside and it burned at first, and I almost stopped, almost screamed, but I knew if I made any noise they would hear, so I just bit my lip really hard. I felt it slide in until it stopped. Then I pulled hard, and it hurt so much my lip began to bleed, and when I looked in the mirror, my teeth were red. Then the blood came, a lot of it. It stopped after a while, after dark, and I bent the hanger and broke it into tiny pieces, and I flushed them down the toilet with all the bloody tissue."

The wad of paper is destroyed now. Molly drops it onto the sidewalk, into the path of the early-afternoon breeze. She is quiet now, looking at the wad roll away, and I don't know what to say, so I move closer to her and put my arms around her, and her warm, wet body begins to shake in her weeping.

"I locked the door to my room," she whispers now, seeing and hearing it all again, it seems, her voice filled with amazement, "and I heard them fighting again. I knew he was beating her, I could actually hear whatever he was using hitting her body, and I shut the blinds and lay down on the bed and put my Walkman on and turned it up as high as it would go. But it didn't do any good. I could still hear her screaming . . ."

"Why did you tell me that?" I ask her much later, still on the bench. The world around where we're sitting hasn't changed too much. The sun has begun to set, so it's not so hot, and in the relief of the afternoon, even more bikers and skaters and joggers are on the road that winds through the park. The sun has spent the hours boiling the air, burning the sweet magnolia smell away. As the St. Charles Avenue traffic gears up, the odor of exhaust takes its place.

"Because I want you to know everything," she says.

"Why?"

"Because we've known each other only a few days."

"I know."

"Because I care about you." She looks at me, then away. "Because I love you," she says.

I look at her face, even though she's searching the ground for the wad, which blew away over an hour ago. With nowhere else to look, she moves her eyes back up to me, and I try my hardest to smile. "You love me," I say. She nods. I say it again.

"I love you," she says slowly, and this time her eyes stay with mine.

Now I look away, at the ground, for that damned wad, at the bikers, the joggers, anything but her face, searching for the answer. More than anything at this moment, I don't want to feel forced into saying anything. I think of the expression on Marian's face when she wants to hear that I love her, and I look back at Molly's face now, through her hair's wisps, at her eyes, and I see a different expression, not one that fits any words, but different. Stronger, maybe; confident? I don't know. Like no matter what I say, her statement will stand as truth, where when Marian says it, the truth of "I love you" rests with my reaction to it. I like this look better. I don't look away again. Instead I say, "I think I love you, too."

I think about that, then say, "No, I'm sorry. That's not right. I love you. I know I do."

Molly's face breaks into a smile, and she puts her arms

around me. We both laugh a little. How short a time it's been, just days, I think.

I look at her eyes again, hoping there's an answer in them, but it isn't clear. All I see is the same thing: She loves me. She's said it, so have I, and I certainly believe it. But is it too soon?

The air is suddenly filled with the combined smells of the afternoon, mostly exhaust, but with a pleasant hint of magnolia, and with the hint of Molly's Tuxedo, and the sweet freshness of her sweat.

"What are you thinking?" she says.

"Nothing important. My mother," and I catch myself too late. It's a lie, but it's the first thing that comes out.

"Your mother? Why?"

"I don't know. I was thinking about when she died."

"She died?"

"When I was eight."

"How?"

"It was an accident," I say. I do not want to talk about this now, I think, I have never talked about it with anyone, not even Carolyn. But I keep talking, probably because Molly has told me everything and I feel I must now tell her something, the one something that means everything. "In her car." I take a deep breath, calling up all the pictures, all the emotions, all that pain, and I see her waiting for me to say it, to get it out.

But I can't.

"It's okay, Deed, you don't have to tell me about it." She leans over and presses her lips to my cheek, then to my lips, and I close my eyes and kiss her back, the first time since the sky ride. I feel some kind of rush inside I never felt before, with anyone. I stop kissing her, just to look at her. She smiles, and I think, This is the same face I saw in the hospital.

"What?"

"Nothing. I was just remembering someone you reminded me of."

"Who?"

"Kate."

She just looks at me and smiles, reinforcing the memory. Then something causes me to look away, and thoughts of my mother flood back into me. "I want to tell you about my mother," I say. "I've never told anyone before, but I want you to know."

She looks at me, and I know she understands what hearing it will mean, that she will be the person who knows me best in the world. Looking at her, it has never been so important to me for anyone to know me the way I want Molly to know me. "I know," I say. "I want to."

I slide closer to her now, and hug her. "She died in an accident." My face behind Molly's, I look away for a moment, and I see my mother's face on every woman walking in the park behind us. I watch them as I talk: "It was on the bridge. It was a weeknight, and she was late. We were all home already, and Mom had a hairdresser appointment across the river. Dad was worried because she was never late. After I was in bed, someone called, I guess the police, and they told him she had died in an accident on the bridge."

I feel her hand on my face, wiping the tears which are hot there. I keep my eyes open, on the women in the park, and the tears overflow from my stinging eyes, to my face. "I wasn't asleep yet, and he began to cry, and I'd never seen that before, and I went out to see what was wrong. I asked him if Mommy was coming home soon, and he told Becky and me that Mommy was gone. He told us she was driving on the bridge, and that someone from the other lane lost control and hit her. She was in the outside lane, against the rail, and the other car forced her against it . . . through it, and she went over . . ."

I lean my head against Molly's, her hand still on my cheek. My eyes fall closed, and I move away from her. Her hands cradle my face, and I put my hands over hers and bury my face in them all. For a moment, I feel a breeze weaving through the trees, and hear the leaves dancing overhead. Then, in the darkness, all I can see is my mother's face that last afternoon, and my father's face, weeping. All I can think of is Molly, and all I can hear are her words "I love you" over and over, and I think about its being too soon, and I think about everything all together, Molly and my mother and all the pictures of her with Dad on their honeymoon and after, later, like in Destin, and how I can just remember the way she laughed, the way her nose wrinkled up and her eyes bunched at the ends, and I can almost remember the way she smelled without perfume, in the mornings, and I feel a pain inside like something has been cut out, and all at once it starts to feel better, but her face doesn't go away, I still see it, I always will, and I feel myself weeping, shaking in Molly's hands, and her lips on my hair, on my forehead, and the warmth of her skin on my face, and I try to feel my mother's hands, I try to smell her perfume now, but it doesn't come, I've lost it, there is only Molly's, Molly, Molly and my mother in the darkness, and then I know it's not too soon, that the wall, my wall, is broken through now, and I am where I want to be, where I have always wanted to be but couldn't, because there was no one to be here with me, and now Molly will be, and I see that it's not too soon, if anything too late, and I lift my face out of Molly's hands, and she is there, her face streaked smooth with tears, she is there, just where I left her, and she loves me, I know she does, and I love her.

TWENTY

At about four I wake up sweaty and shaking from a nightmare, probably the one thing I'd have thought I'd be safe from, tonight. How can a person discover he's in love in the afternoon, then dream a nightmare only a few hours later?

The thing I hate about dreams—well, *my* dreams—is that I never see myself. What I see, all I see, is my own point of view. I suppose my dreams give me the same perspective I get in a movie, or in life. Yes, exactly: I'm a powerless bystander, an observer. Right away, it creates frustration, an instant panic.

Chip was at the Grill, at the counter, his face a blank white, his fingernails leaking blood, which spread in a shiny nail-polish puddle on the Formica. And I was on the seat right next to him, my hand on his shoulder, saying, "Chip." He turned to me and his eyes bulged open, and their color went from blue to black, like someone had squirted ink into them. He just stared at me, through me, then took a finger and traced it across the counter, through the fresh blood. When he brought his finger up to somewhere between our faces, it wasn't covered with blood, but with a white powder. And all around his nose, I saw, were white flecks. Then he put his finger under his nose and sniffed all the coke away. Looking back at me, he quickly wiped away the dusty flecks.

Then he smiled at me, and I looked away, back to the counter, where a tiny river of blood had meandered to the far edge, where it cascaded out of sight.

"Come on, Deed," he said then. When I saw his face, all the color was there again, that café-au-lait color, and he was sucking on his coke-snort finger. Making a slurping sound, he took it slowly out of his mouth, trailing a line of sticky red after it, on his bottom lip; he licked it away. As he stood up, looking much taller than he ever was, he pressed the finger to my lips. I tried to turn my head away, but couldn't. He snaked his index finger into my mouth, and I tasted blood. When I stood to meet his height, my nose began to burn. Instinctively, I used my hand to wipe it as if I had a cold, and when I glanced at my fingers, they were flecked with the same white powder.

"Come on, Deed," Chip said again, and turned away from me.

I'm at Carolyn's by ten-thirty, as scheduled. When I walk quickly through the waiting room, past the frosted-glass windows leading to the receptionist's cubicle, I remember the first time I was here. I wonder if she still pencils me in . . .

"Then the scene changed," I tell Carolyn, trying to recall every detail of the dream. "It was strange. As clear as the Grill was, the new place wasn't. It wasn't exactly dark, but it was . . . cloudy. And wet. Like, underground. There were tunnels everywhere, leading away in all directions, into the dark. Somehow, the light was always with us, somewhere behind me. It made long shadows in front of me, and in front of Chip. We walked and walked, until we came to a door. Chip said, 'Deed, remember the Grill?' I said, 'Yes.' And he said, 'Good. Remember it well.' Then he opened the door, and he was gone, and *I* was in the room, which was white, white like a bathroom, and the sink was filled with red drops. When I looked down at my wrist, it was healed, like it is now. But my fingers, my fingers . . . wept blood."

She says to tell her about Chip. I tell her what I can, about how we met on the streetcar, about his family's history, even the night at Café du Monde when we tried to match the café au lait to his skin. The day he died at the Grill.

Eventually, she asks me if I've ever done cocaine, if I've ever done it with Chip. I tell her yes.

"Did he work?" she asks.

"I don't think so. I mean, we only saw each other at night, never in the daytime, and I never met any of his friends. I don't know what he did when he wasn't with me."

I thought it was odd that he never talked about anything else. It was always *Remember the night we . . . ?* or something like that. Never the present, always the past, with him. He really was a loner, as far as I knew, and I got the impression somehow that he never liked knowing too many people at once. He once said he liked to take the world on one person at a time. At least, I think he said it; maybe I thought it.

"If he didn't work," she says, "then how could he afford the cocaine?"

I don't know what to say. She's right. I didn't think to ask him, ever. He got it, that was all I knew, and I didn't like it. The truth was, I didn't *want* to know how he got it, or where, or about what he had to do to get it. If Chip wanted to keep this part of his life away from me, I didn't care at all. I didn't want to know about it.

I say that now; then: "Oh, I know what you're thinking, you're thinking he was a dealer."

"Do you think so?"

"I guess it's possible, sure. Like I said, he never talked about much, really. Just things that didn't mean much to either of us, like music, maybe, or sex. You know. Everything was a game to him, he never took anything too seriously." I think about this a second, then say, "Well, no, that's not right. It's not that he didn't take it seriously, it's that he didn't dwell on anything very long. He took everything in stride. Sometimes it seemed like he was bored with everything. That's really the way it was. The truth is, we were good friends, but I didn't know much about him. Nothing, really."

"Did he ever talk about dying?"

"Dying? Yeah, once. Strange, it was the last time we were out together. We were at Pat O'Brien's and I asked him if he was afraid to die. I was thinking about Jason, and it just seemed like a good thing to ask. I don't know why. But he said, I remember, he said, 'There's too much else.' "

" 'Too much else'?"

"I guess too much else to think about."

"Mm-hmm. What did he say after that?"

What *did* he say after that? "Nothing," I suddenly recall. "We were interrupted by a couple of girls who came and sat down at the table."

"Too bad."

"I wish I knew for sure what he meant, what he was going to say. 'There's too much else.' "

"You said he OD'd. How do you know that?"

"Well," I say, thinking, "I don't. But his *face* was so white, and he was sweaty, and his skin was burning up. He barely recognized me."

She nods a little. She takes out a Camel and rolls it around in her fingers.

"I guess we can be sure your friend had a whole life you didn't know about. We'll never know for sure, but I'd say he was addicted to cocaine and dealt so he could afford it himself. And from what you say, overdose sounds right."

"What did the dream mean?"

"Don't you know?" She pulls a dry drag from the cigarette, then relaxes her hand on the armrest of her chair.

Looking over at the colors in the Agam, I think about the dream a minute. Blood. Coke. Chip's life. My death. The bathroom. Underground.

"Don't you?" she asks again.

"I think so. I think it was something I knew, sort of, but never thought about. I never *wanted* to think about it, like I said. Chip's addiction was what kept him alive, all the time I knew him. It also killed him. Cocaine was his blood, and his blade. Like mine—but worse."

Carolyn looks at me thoughtfully, one eyebrow raised in an arc. Slowly, her face bobs in a nod. She pulls another drag from the Camel. She gets up and walks over to the window. The city below is pretty busy; it's just after lunch, and everyone is hurrying back to work.

Looking out at the city, she says, "Maybe." In a minute, she turns, her eyes resting for a moment on the girl in the wheat field.

Walking around later, I realize it's a week until Mardi Gras. I wonder which images will present themselves to me that day. What forms will Jason's face take?

For just a moment I think of Lynn Waters. Her boyfriend rejected her, the way I'm rejecting Marian. But I know Marian won't commit suicide, I just know. She's not the—

I guess Lynn's death is particularly useful right now: It

shows where I've come from, what I avoided, and also where, I suppose, I could end up, if I'm not careful.

The pink sun floats just over the city this afternoon, a fiery ball promising warmth and destruction at once. On the ground, here, it's rush hour. Above, the sky shimmers in the sun's winter heat, and a slightly cool breeze makes the city sway in the rhythm of the night's coming parade. Mardi Gras brings with it a new pace to the city, an expectation, an early end to every day, a much-needed release in the form of the constant tribal screaming to the floats in the dark.

TWENTY-ONE

After lunch at Rascal's, Molly and I take the streetcar to her street, and she gets off. The stop at Milan Street is where I need to jump off to go to Carolyn's office, but I get off sooner, so I can walk. I need some time to think about Jason, to get things straight. He's on my mind today more than usual, probably because Mardi Gras is coming. Actually, it couldn't be anything else. Today, I think, will be a good day to talk about him. For some reason, all I can focus on is a night we spent joyriding in his father's Olds, in the rain. What a night . . .

"Wait," he said. We'd just taken the car onto I-10 and been stunned by the effect of water over us at a hundred miles an hour. I was standing on the street, at around three-thirty in the morning, and the rain was falling gently, like a spring shower. We'd been out for a while, and I wanted to go inside and dry off. But Jason said, "Wait," and walked over and put his arms around me. It was electric, that moment, as illuminating and as blinding as the storm's flashes.

That's what's on my mind.

There was no describing it, there was no category for it, no compartment to fit it into among the range of emotions men are supposed to feel for one another. It cemented our friendship, but it also made us brothers. After that, nothing could have split us. We were nearly one person. There was love, and more. I never could find a word to use for it. Now I think maybe there just *isn't* a word, because if there were, then maybe it wouldn't have been so extraordinary. Maybe it was a truly new experience. After that night, that was always the way it was, until the night I found him dead.

". . . until the night I found him dead."

For a few minutes, Carolyn doesn't say anything. I know my new story has impressed her, as it impressed me—when it happened.

I look around the room, and when my eyes land on the girl in the wheat field, for the first time I fully identify with her looking back, looking back at where she's been, where she came from. It's almost like now she understands things a little better.

It all comes back to perspective, I think.

"You know, one thing strikes me about that night," she says.

"What is it?"

"It's what you said about feeling free, out in the storm. I don't know why, but I like it. There's something . . . right about it."

I smile at her then.

"Is that something you used to think about a lot?"

"What?"

"Freedom?"

"Yeah, all the time. I still do."

"In what way?"

"For starters," I say, "I know that if most people heard

that story, they'd certainly think we were crazy right off the bat. Jason and I never told anyone about that night. In fact, I've never mentioned it to anyone until today. Somehow, I knew you'd understand."

"You did?"

"Sure. *Don't* you?"

"I think so. But I want you to explain it."

"Which part?"

"The part about freedom."

"Well, you know about when I was growing up, how all the guys at Newman thought I was a fag because I didn't play football. That's how it starts. It starts when we're little boys. We're taught to compete, to excel, to be faster, stronger, braver. We're taught not to feel anything except glory. We're taught not to love anything except a perfect touchdown, or a home run. So we grow up missing something that girls have. We don't *know* we're missing it, but we are. There must be others like me, though, who discover it and hold on to it before it's too late, but I don't think there are many. Anyway, then boys grow up and have families, and teach their sons the same crap all over again. They never show any emotion, like hugging their sons, or kissing them. Everything is measured in how far you can throw a football. And that's wrong. There's more to it than that."

"And so if men teach their sons to be more emotional, it'll get better?"

"Probably not. I don't know what anybody can do. But something has to be done. When Jason and I were standing in that storm, we weren't really doing anything wrong. I mean, there's a whole set of things men are allowed to do, but after that, there's nothing. It's that way, or else. What Jason and I had that night was exciting. How often do men get to be in that situation and not be laughed at? There was something about that night that made it okay to just be ourselves, you know? No images, no crap. Just truth. Just people. You see?"

"I think so." She looks at me for a few moments, a smile slowly growing on her lips. "I have a question," she says, and I get the feeling the question's a heavy one because the smile falls away.

I don't say anything.

Finally, she asks, "How did Jason die?"

No one's asked it before. No one's forced me to think about it, to grapple with it, no one's put me into this position, until now.

For a little while I don't say anything to her. Jason's face —before that night—appears somewhere between my chair and Carolyn's. He's laughing, that night in the rain. That night keeps returning to me. His mouth is wide in joy; too soon, the image fades into another of his recurring faces, his mouth spread this time in death—the bathroom.

"He died in his shower," I say. Her eyes shoot back to me, as if this is exactly what she wanted to hear, like it fits some puzzle she couldn't finish alone.

"In his shower?"

"Yeah. He . . . sort of hung himself."

Carolyn straightens herself in her seat, leaning forward. "Go on."

"I don't really know too much. I found him on the floor, and he was already dead. There was some blood, and a rope."

"And he was nude?"

I nod; then: "The end of the rope was still in the shower, in the water." I don't know why this thought occurs to me. For some reason I think it's important that she know this, that she somehow see this with me. "The water was pink, from the blood. And the rope was blotchy with it."

"He was in the shower when you found him?"

"Uh-uh. On the floor. I guess he fell, or collapsed, or something."

I see him there again, eyes staring, mouth screaming without a sound. His arm— "His arm was behind his head, like he was scratching his neck. The rope was still tight, and his fingers were stuck in the coils."

"Wait a minute. What did he hang himself on? Where was the rod?"

"There wasn't a rod. It's a stall shower, with a glass door."

"So how did he do it? Did he use his own hands to do it?"

"I guess. He was already dead, Carolyn, I—"

"Was it a suicide?"

"Sure."

She stands up and walks over to her bookcase. She runs a fingernail across the spines of the hardbacks, and it makes a clicking sound, nail against leather. From there, not finding the book she wants, she says, "It could have been an accident, Deed."

"No. No, it couldn't have been. He was depressed that night," I say. I tell her about Barbara and the gang and about there being a guy at Barbara's to see him pick her up, and how one would be at the restaurant, and about the gang bang at the Butterfly. ". . . But she wasn't even there when he went to get her. And whoever was watching saw that. It was over before it began. He knew he was finished. It was his last chance to be *in,* and he'd lost it."

"And then?" She comes back to her chair and sits.

"He called me, and he sounded okay, a little shook up. I told him we'd go to the Grill—"

"The Grill?"

"Camellia Grill," I say, "to celebrate. He laughed a little, and I said I'd be there at nine. When I got there, no one answered, and the door swung open and I went up and found him in his bathroom, dead."

"I'm . . . so sorry, Deed."

I just look at her. Quick, painful flashes of that night blink before me. Eyes, rope, water—rope, mirror, mouth.

"And you think it was suicide?"

"Don't you?"

She stares at me now, waiting. I can practically see her answer weighed. Then, suddenly, it's: "No. It could have been something else, an accident. It's called autoerotic asphyxia."

"Auto *what?*"

"Autoerotic asphyxia."

"What's that?" I lean forward now. I am suddenly intrigued. I've been so sure about Jason since I found him. But he wasn't the type, I know that. And now—an accident? This, this auto thing?

"It's a . . . a condition, I suppose that's the right word for it. You, you strangle yourself while you masturbate, and the danger, the excitement—it makes the orgasm better. At least, that's what they say."

"And you think Jason did that with the rope?"

"Maybe. Many teen suicides—boys, mostly—are really accidental. Autoerotic asphyxia. I don't know the numbers, my volume on it is gone. But it's significant, I know."

I just look at her.

"Look at it this way for a minute, okay? You've told me about Jason before. About your childhood, about the way he—what?—the way he catapulted himself off the swings. The way he drove that night in the storm. The way he defied the boys in grade school to be your pal. I mean, from what you say, Jason had a reckless streak. Maybe there was something you didn't know about. Maybe another part of that streak was . . . sexual. Usually, boys practice that kind of thing more than once. They become good at it, until that one time they screw up, or lose control. I don't know for sure, Deed, but maybe that was the night he lost control."

I just breathe.

"You think so?" she asks.

"I . . . Maybe. Maybe. I guess it could have been like that. Everything you just said—Green Trees, that night. It's all true. I never thought of it like that before. He was pretty daring. Maybe he did this thing you're talking about."

"It's really bothered you, hasn't it, thinking he committed suicide?"

"It bothered me that he *died.* I just assumed it was suicide. I never thought it was an accident. I didn't know it *could* be." I look at her for a moment. "Maybe it was."

"You know," she says, "I think there are two kinds of suicides. There are people who really want to die. They've thought it over, and they've made conscious decisions. And then they wreck their cars, they jump off buildings or bridges or out of windows, or they shoot themselves. Something unstoppable. They *commit* suicide. Then there's a group who want to escape, who are depressed, who just need a break for a while, and they think dying is the answer, that it's the easy way out. And they try to drown, like Kate, or do some damage with a razor blade, or take pills, whatever. They do things that can be stopped, they do things where people can find them. These people *attempt* suicide. And, Deed, there's a difference—a vast difference—between the two types. From what I know about Jason, from you, I don't think he fit either type. It doesn't come together correctly. From what *you* know of him, and about suicide, everything, do you really think he killed himself on purpose?"

I sit there, amazed at the speed of my answer. Perhaps I have always known it, but had no explanation to back it up. But now, it all fits. And it feels a little easier to accept this solution. I don't know why. I know I miss him as much, probably more. It's easier—but sadder.

Before I leave, Carolyn asks me if I'd like to have dinner with her. We decide to go out to the lake, to Fitzgerald's. She tells me she has to make a couple of calls, and to wait for her in the outer office.

After dinner, she hands me a couple of sheets of paper from her purse.

"These are some of the things I read to myself when I need strength," she says. "They all really go with what we were talking about this afternoon. Some came from people I know, some from books and other places. You know the Wordsworth . . ."

I read over the list, coming to names I don't know. "Who wrote, 'Write your own lines, write your own play, be your own author, be your own authority'?"

"An old teacher of mine. It was from a course on feminism. One of those, the one I say is from my grandmother . . ?"

"Here: ' 'Tis not life that matters, but the courage you bring to it.' "

"That's not hers. I think Somerset Maugham wrote it, but she used to say it to me all the time."

"Who's Ayn Rand?"

"Oh, she's someone I used to love in college. She wrote a book called *The Fountainhead,* which is what that quote is from. In the book, the quote means something else, because of the context, but apart, it's really something special, and very wise, I think."

" 'There's nothing as significant as a human face. Nor as eloquent. We can never really know another person, except by our first glance at him. Because, in that glance, we know everything. Even though we're not always wise enough to unravel the knowledge.' "

TWENTY-TWO

My dad and I have breakfast again at the Grill a couple of days later. We have a good talk, all about Molly. It seems there's nothing but Molly on my mind right now, so it doesn't take much pushing to get me to start yapping. I think it takes him by surprise, I talk so much; it's the first time in so long that I've wanted to. He asks about Carolyn, and Kate, and "How is all of that going?" and I tell him a little about Jane and Lynn. He seems interested in me now, and I think back to what he told me the other day. He really wants to know about my life outside our house, the house where I was born, where Becky was born, where our mother died. He says he remembers reading something about Buddy Waters, Lynn's father, in the paper recently. "Something about tax evasion, I think."

For the first time in a long while, but maybe just for the first time, I feel at ease with him, that I can more or less be myself with him. Now, I am not afraid of him, of what he knows, of how he can use it, not against me, but on me. It occurs to me that he has changed as much as I have since the nights I saw him cry, from the first time to the second, from then to now.

I tell him so. He asks how I've changed, and I tell him my outlook. I tell him the future looks a lot brighter, which it does, that I know something good lies around the corner. He smiles, says he used to say that, "around the corner," when he was a boy.

I apologize to him for doing what I did; he tells me he's sorry for not doing more of what he should have to prevent it. Neither of us mentions Frankie, which is probably best for right now. When I tell him that many things went into my decision, that it wasn't just him, he suggests that we sit down and talk about the things that made me do it. I agree that, eventually, we could.

Before we know it, I have to be at Carolyn's. We walk out into the most gorgeous morning I can remember. Clear blue sky, not a cloud in it, the unmistakable scent of magnolias, and a cool Dixie breeze. When the word comes to mind, "Dixie," so does Chip. This time, his image does not upset me. I know if he were here, he wouldn't let anything get him down; he'd spend the day at the Butterfly, catching the rays on his skateboard, shirt off, in shorts: his uniform for days like this. He once took me with him; he was the oldest 'boarder there.

When Dad pulls the car up to the front of Carolyn's building, I look over at him. I see the sparkle in his eye from when I was a little boy, before everything, and I see that I look a little like him. If my head were balding a little, if my features were a little more rounded, then maybe . . . I lean over and kiss him goodbye. I'd nearly forgotten what that was like. "See you later," I say, and get out.

I walk into Carolyn's office and they're all there. Kate, Molly, Carolyn. The women in my life.

We all sit down, and I tell them my father and I had breakfast at the Grill again, and that things between us are improving.

"Have you forgiven him?" Carolyn asks.

"For his affair? No," I say. Carolyn smiles a little. I look at Molly and tell her quickly about my father's affair with Frankie.

"You say no, Deed, but you seem to have," says Carolyn. "You talk about it fairly calmly. Did you hear yourself just now, telling Molly? 'My dad had an affair with a girl I was dating.' That sounds fairly nonchalant, if you ask me. Yet you say you haven't forgiven him."

"I guess it looks like I have, but I haven't. I don't think I ever can."

"But you're getting along so well now, right?"

"Yeah, but it's different. I can't forgive him, and I can't forgive Frankie. They *lied* to me."

"Everybody does, eventually," she says. "It's inevitable." I can't believe she's saying this to me now.

"Will you?"

"I don't think I will."

"Will Molly, or Kate?"

"I don't know. I can't know. But neither can they. Things happen, and you try to avoid hurting people too much, and sometimes a lie is better."

"Not in this case. Not with my dad and Frankie."

"Why not?"

"They betrayed me. I *trusted* them both with . . . with my life. And they treated me like shit. It was like, for six months my father forgot I was his son! I can't just forget it ever happened. I can't."

"Can't? Or won't?"

Some thought, then: "Won't. I have to make sure it never happens again."

"Then why try to get along at all?"

"Shouldn't I get along with him? He's my father."

"Lots of people don't talk to their fathers. You can, too."

I wait a few seconds before I say anything, watching her closely. "But I *want* to get along with him. Don't you understand?"

"No. *Why?* If he hurt you so deeply, if he betrayed you like you say, then why?"

"Because he's my father. I know that sounds stupid, but it's the truth. That's it. The whole point is to find the truth, right? Well, that's the truth. I love him. He's a good man, despite it all. He makes mistakes, so do I. The man's my father. That may just be a rationalization, but I can't help it."

What's with her today? She can't be serious about all this, she can't expect me to have any other answer for her. She's just playing with me, maybe, or is she pushing me to make sure I really believe what I'm telling her? If that *is* what she's doing, it worked.

Or is it something totally different? Maybe today's just the wrong day for this. Maybe this is a hot button for her, one that I can't push now. Who knows? What has she left me to say but "Hey, *your* mother's gone. What would you do if you were in my position?"

The moment I say it, I know it was a mistake. But instantly, I see the eyes in the room go to her.

Slowly, Carolyn says, "I . . ." But that's all.

"Carolyn, I think you have to answer Deed's question," Kate says. "You've never backed away before, not from any of us. You can't do it now."

Carolyn stares at Kate, wide-eyed, not quite able to swallow this . . . mutiny?

"No," I say, "she doesn't have to."

"She does, Deed. Wait a minute."

"Deed, that's how the group works," Molly says. "We're *all* in the group, even Carolyn."

"I know, but—"

"Okay," Carolyn says then. "Okay." She looks at each

of us, waiting a few seconds on each of our faces, first Kate, then Molly, then me. Then she glances over at the old photograph of her mother.

"I have a question for all of you," she says. She waits a moment, and the room is quiet. The last time it was this quiet, there was only the sound of the hum of the stereo, after the taped message from Lynn's boyfriend. My eyes are fixed on Carolyn's face, waiting. I see by her look that all the others' are, too. Suddenly she snaps out of the trance she had fallen into.

"What is suicide?" she asks us.

We all look at her, then at each other, maybe looking for an answer, and she goes on.

"What is it? Do any of you know? Can you explain it to me? Kate? Molly?" She looks at me, then says, "Deed? Do you know? Two of you have attempted suicide. Lynn Waters attempted once, then tried it again and made it. Deed, you've heard the tape which pushed her out of her bedroom window. Kate, Molly, if you want to hear it, just let me know."

"Carolyn, what—"

"Wait a moment, Kate. Just wait, all of you. Let me finish, all right?" No one challenges her this time.

"When Lynn jumped out of her window, she made a choice. She made a choice to stop her life. Now, to me, *that* was the suicide. Not when she died, but the *decision* to die. Two of you have also made that decision, and something saved you, I don't know what. But you made the decision to stop living, for whatever reason. So I ask again, what is suicide? I'll tell you what *I* think it is. I think that each of you has a question, one question, that you don't ever want to answer. It's probably a question you can't answer, and if you could, it would change your life. One minute, things are this way, and the next, they're that way—all because you answered the question. Sometimes you don't even need to know the answer; just *asking* the question will change everything. Let's call it, the question, let's call it a trigger. Now, I think we all have triggers. Each person has one, which means that each person is capable of suicide. That makes sense to me, given the wide range of people who commit suicide, or try to. Suicide is not limited by age, by race, by class, or by income. It's something which is a possible choice for every person on earth. It's a disease. I think that every person, faced with his or her trigger, would at the very least *think* about suicide. Studies show that nearly everyone has at least thought about it at one time or another. Sometimes more than once. Sometimes every day. Yet they never do it, they don't go through with it. Why? . . . Now, the tricky thing about triggers is that they're all different—and they change. A trigger you have today might not be the same in a year—or tomorrow. Who knows? So all of you may think about suicide every morning, yet you may never try it again. But one day, you might find yourself face to face with your trigger, and you're going to have to decide. Suicide is a choice you make, it's a decision. You either face your trigger and defeat it, or you do something you think isn't as bad—you die. Or, the other way, you either commit suicide or you face something which, in *your* mind, is much worse—living with the question, or the answer, the truth. That's what suicide is, to me. Deed, Molly, Kate—it's a choice you make between two extremes, and the best and the worst of the two, how you choose which is which, is up to you. Deed, when you were in that bathroom, you came face to face with your trigger. Kate, you faced yours at the pool. Molly . . ."

Carolyn looks at Molly closely. Molly, whose eyes are on Carolyn, frozen, mesmerized, suddenly becomes aware that we are all looking at her, and she looks at me.

"Molly," Carolyn says, "you came face to face with yours six years ago."

"What?"

"You did. I've wanted to try and show you that."

"What do you mean?" She looks from me to Carolyn, then back again.

"I mean, I'm not sure your abortion wasn't a suicide attempt."

The room is instantly charged. Molly is on her feet, and I feel that she is desperate for space, for air. I stand up—

"Sit down, Deed."

"Why? She needs—"

Molly's eyes dart around the room. Her breathing has changed, becoming quicker and panicky. Even Kate shifts in her chair.

"She needs to find the truth. She has to do it alone, she has to be alone with it, Deed. You can't help her."

I do not sit down, but stand there, my eyes on Molly. Her body shivers, as if something were hitting her again and again. Then I realize that something *is* hitting her. It's the trigger. I suddenly feel this rage toward Carolyn, who is completely different today. She's a stranger to me today, and it's odd, and uncomfortable. Everyone can see it. I could understand her playing devil's advocate for a while, before maybe, but now? "How can you do this to her? You said she was fragile, and you do this to her! You push her right up against what made her choose before. Look at her! What do you think her choice will be now?" I run to Molly, my arms out—

"—Deed, don't—"

I get there, near the window, near the Agam, when Molly turns to me—

"—don't—"

"—Deed—"

"—Molly—"

"—Stop it! Get away from me! All of you!" Molly looks at us all, all standing now, tensed, ready to rescue her from . . . "Carolyn's right. I have to do this alone. I have to answer the question. Now, everyone, sit down. Please. I'm okay."

Molly's voice is calm, eerie, different than I've ever heard it before. We all slowly come off our edges, onto our chairs. Kate is the last one standing, and she looks only at Molly.

She says softly, "Molly, I agree with you. Carolyn's right. You do have to do it yourself. We all do. We all need to be alone and figure this out for ourselves. But, Molly darling, you have all the time you need, you don't have to do it now."

Then Molly smiles at Kate, and for a moment it seems as if they are sisters, or best friends, the same age, Molly's. Kate seems like a child in this calm. It's a creepy feeling, but familiar. I have felt it before, I realize, every time I have ever been with Kate. This is the feeling I had when I saw her for the first time, in the hospital. And when I saw Kate's unbelievable youth in Molly's laughter.

"Kate," Carolyn says, nearly whispering.

"But I've already done it," Molly says, her eyes locked with Kate's. "I know the answer. I know what I was doing when I did what I did. I know what I was thinking. It's okay. It's okay. I didn't want to die. I never thought of dying. I wanted to be alive, but without the baby. I did not want to commit suicide."

I glance over at Carolyn, and I see in her a response she doesn't give. I know she'd say Molly never would have thought she was committing suicide, not under those conditions, and not now, looking back. I know this, I think, because I believe it. It makes sense. I also know I will never talk about it, because all that really matters is that Molly *believes* she wasn't committing suicide, that she faced her trigger and survived; as long as she believes her truth, that's what's important.

Slowly, Kate and Molly hug each other, and Molly closes her eyes, which tells me she feels safe, that she's content. When Molly sits back down, next to me now, Kate remains by the window, looking out. In the distance, the Superdome is bright in the afternoon sun, like an alien ship from light-years away.

Kate turns away from the window. "I have something to say. I've been doing some thinking about things, and I have an answer that may help someone here. Carolyn, you tell me—what should I do? Should I share it or not?"

"By all means, share it. That's why we're here, Kate, you know that."

"I only hesitate because we've all decided it's important to make these decisions, discoveries maybe, for ourselves. I don't want to intrude upon anyone's choices."

"Well, I certainly think it's all right. Right?" Carolyn asks both of us. We both give the go-ahead, anxious to hear what it is Kate has to say.

Kate walks around the room, looking from the art to us, from us to the art. We wait for her to say something, at this point anything, and the room grows electric again.

Then Kate says, "Deed, this is about you."

I see Kate's eyes are on me. She walks over to me, sits on the wide arm of the chair. She holds one of my hands. Hers are cold with old age.

"Deed once told me he used to wish a truck would hit him," she says. All at once, I am completely embarrassed, even here, in this company. I look only at the floor, at the footprint pattern in the carpet. The skin on the back of my neck begins to burn.

"When he told me that, we had just met, and I honestly didn't know what to think. I thought it was sad. Gruesome. He said he wanted to feel something. He told me he wanted to know how it felt to be slapped, or how it felt to be on fire. He said . . . he said he wanted a truck to hit him and throw him forward, so he could feel that."

I feel only one thing now, everyone's eyes on me.

"There's one thing I know Deed knows how to feel, and that's love. One of his worries is that he hasn't felt it yet. I thought to tell him he has a while to go, but then I discovered he *has* felt it. It's just that he's only felt the other side, the side that's painful. We've all felt it. For Deed, it came from betrayal, and from dishonesty. Deed's wish to be hit by a truck, or to burn, tells me something. I know you can't know this, Carolyn, unless he's told you about the truck."

"He hasn't."

"Well, then all of this is new to everyone. Deed, I want you to stop wishing to be hit, or burned. Or anything like that."

The force of her voice makes me look up, finally, at her. She is looking right at me, her faded blue eyes as clear as a crystal ball that tells the future. My own eyes ask one question: Why?

"What *I* think, is that you've already been hit. The truck you want is really your own life. Whatever made you go into that bathroom and cut your wrist—that was your truck."

I begin to see something I've wanted to see for . . . forever, it seems. Its brightness grows by the second, so quickly that I can barely think of words to say, to tell her that she's right.

"You have met your own life head-on, and you may have tripped a little, but you came back, like you said you wanted to, remember? You lived, finally. Am I making any sense?"

"Yes. One hundred percent perfect sense" is what I manage to say, and when it comes, it comes as a whisper, as a reaction to a direct question, not really as a thoughtful answer.

I hear, "Yes, Kate, you are," from Carolyn. "It's true, Deed."

"I know." I look only at Kate. "It's so clear now, all of it. Sitting here, I was trying to come up with a question, a trigger. But you found it for me."

Immediately, the room relaxes for the second time in one session. The air feels weightless, for the first time in . . .

"The question for me was . . . everything together. It was growing up, it was my mother, my father, Frankie, Jason, Chip—the whole thing. I know the question, even the words. Am I willing to go on with things the way they are? Even if I don't have the love I want? Am I ready to take another step forward only to receive a blow that'll send me two steps back? Before, I wasn't. That was my answer. But now"—I look at Molly, then at Kate—"now I am. Now I *want* to move forward, I want to go somewhere, I want what I have now, whatever and however it is."

I have crashed into my life, and survived. That, I know, is something I will always have, and just *knowing* it will get me through anything.

Carolyn tells us to take a break. While we're all eating the Tastee doughnuts from the box near the coffee maker, Carolyn takes me aside and tells me she's sorry for pushing so hard. When I ask her why she did, she says that it's because the Board has been pushing her to do something about the group's future. She says the pressure is too great right now. Somehow, though, I feel like there's more to it, and I say so.

"There *is* more. And believe it or not, it has to do with what you asked me about. It's my father. There's . . . It's just difficult for me to talk about. Can you understand that?"

"Yeah, sure, you know I can. But it might help to talk, to let it out."

Hearing that, she laughs a little at her own words spoken back to her. She doesn't say anything more, just looks at me, like a professor might look at a student who has finally become an expert in the field. It's a strange look.

I take her hand and squeeze once, then walk over to Molly, on the other side of the room.

"There was a time," Carolyn says to us, "when I faced a trigger. I think that's why I know about them so well. I've faced more than one, to tell the truth. And every once in a while, I have to face one again, on certain days. Like today. My trigger involves this group, and why I formed it in the first place. I think you all know that my mother died when I was born, and that my dad raised me. And that's where all this comes from. It just wasn't the way . . . the way I think it should have been, growing up. I don't feel up to going into detail right now, I'm sorry. Please understand this is something I have to work on by myself. I shouldn't let it interfere with anything we discuss in group. I can tell you that, like you, I have had hard times. Maybe part of what makes this group work is that I really empathize with each of you, deeper than you know. Though the specifics may be different, the feelings, the emotions, are the same. And the triggers have the same effect. They turned my life upside down, too. They still do. I don't want to blame him, but a big cause for all this is my father. Our relationship has been quite destructive over the years, and there have been times we haven't spoken. But like I said, I can't blame him for it all. I wasn't really the model daughter, and I wasn't the son he wanted. Mostly, I wasn't my mother, and he just didn't know the first thing about raising a daughter all by himself. We can certainly talk about this if you want to, but I hope that we can do it another day. All right?"

My eyes are on her, have been since she started speaking. We are all standing, still, at points around the room. I am standing with Molly, near the window.

Finally, Kate says, "Carolyn, I think we all understand. I'm sorry for pushing you the way I did."

"No, please, you were right to push. That's why we're here."

The only thing Carolyn has not mentioned is her own suicide attempt, something I guess only I know about, pretty much by accident. I decide it's a secret I must keep.

Before we leave, she tells us that the Board has demanded a forum to discuss the future of the group. Carolyn says she hasn't got one idea about what to do, and she asks for our help. Without saying a word, we all realize the weight of the problem. All of us have come to depend on each other, and on Carolyn's guidance, as others will. This group is as much our family as our real families are.

She tells us the Board has scheduled a meeting for Wednesday to discuss the fate of the Suicide Counseling Group. Kate volunteers to write a short speech, which is just about what we all would expect of her, under these circumstances. We all agree to be there Wednesday, for support. We decide together that we must present ideas which will keep the group alive.

Molly suggests we let the general public know we exist *before* they have to make their choices, before, as she says, "they pull their triggers," and just as she says it, she smiles, knowing it was the wrong choice of words. Maybe instead of counseling survivors, she says, we should concentrate on saving lives we might lose. Thinking of Jason, and even Chip, I add my support to her suggestion. Because in the line drawn between this choice and that choice, it occurs to me that most people will choose suicide as the easier, the best, route. Maybe they wouldn't if they saw that the line was a dotted one.

TWENTY-THREE

I meet Kate at the Audubon Zoo for lunch. The last time I was here was before they renovated it, before they took all the metal bars out and put the animals into cageless neighborhoods. Now it's like you can almost touch them while you talk to them.

If today had a color, it would have to be gray. There is no blue in the sky today, only a blanket of gloom over the city. From far away comes a breeze, coldish and wet. It flaps scarves and coats like flags on their poles, like on a windy summer afternoon. The scent of winter rain hangs in the air like burnt rubber—ugly and threatening and bursting with memory. But the threat itself is a bluff, the rain doesn't come. The icy air is a shock to the city, even now, when other cities are buried under feet of snow. The news programs are preoccupied with the question of Mardi Gras: Will it be cold and rainy, or better? It seems worse is impossible. The gloom dampens the revelry of carnival. Even Kate seems under the spell of the gray, her overcoat buttoned around her, and a scarf wrapped around her neck. For me, there's just a sweater; it is so seldom really cold here that when it is, I like to take advantage of it. All my life, walking in the cold has cleansed me. I believe it's the crisp air, the sharp bite of the wind. Today, I'm a little tired because another parade, Hermes, was last night. Though I was alone, it was fun. Images of Jason didn't bombard me, but they threatened. Only Kate and Molly and this chill could get me out of bed this early. It seems the lack of the sun and heat intrigues the animals, because they are out, playing in the cold. Perhaps the animals and I have something in common.

We're near the orangutans, and they're looking at us. They look like they understand what we're saying, maybe even what we're thinking, like they want to add something, some thought. I want them to. In the middle of this staring contest, the large one pads over to a thick rope tied between two trees and hoists himself up onto it. He sits there, half on the rope, half on a tall stump, looking back at us. His mate sits where she has been all along. Another fifteen feet and I could put my hand out and touch her.

Later, walking, we pass the giraffes, and I remember being here with my parents, and my father lifting me in his arms up high, high enough to feed the giraffe a small fistful of grass.

To get back across the zoo to the seals, Kate and I pass the primates again. This time we go by the chimpanzees. My mother adored the chimps, like the orangs (I suddenly remember), and I notice that all the chimps are staring at me, as if on the verge of a sentence. I think, They recognize my face, they remember me being here with my mother, they know who I am and that I loved them with her a long time ago. I still love you, I think at them, I still love you.

The seals are kept in a large concrete structure that looks like a Greek temple on a hill in Athens, except there's not one hill to be found in New Orleans. The temple hasn't changed in all these years, since I was a boy. When we get there, though, the pool has been drained and the seals are gone. There is no trace of them. The bottom of the pool is scraped and stained with rust and algae.

"I used to bring my grandson here," Kate says, her hand on the decorative iron bars surrounding the pool. In the center is an island of boulders; the seals used to paddle up close to it and jump up, then waddle around in the sun. "We used to come here every afternoon to watch them feed the seals."

I think about how so many things have changed since I was a boy, and that I am still a boy in so many ways, too many. I can remember being little in so many pairs of arms, my father's, my mother's, my grandmother's, all in this zoo, all long ago.

I think now that I don't speak to my grandmother often enough; what a shame all these years have been wasted between us. It seems to me that if I can mend the break with my father, I can surely bridge the ravine between him and my grandmother. They may not like each other, but like it or not, they are family. I know his argument by heart now, that any connection they had died on the bridge eleven years ago. But he is wrong, he will have to understand that he is wrong, that this is another thing he considers unimportant which I consider not only important but vital. The connection he has to her is twofold. Becky and me. His blood is forever mixed with hers, through our mother, in us. That's family. That's something I will have to make them *both* understand. I promise myself that I will call her soon, right after Mardi Gras.

"My grandmother used to bring me here, too," I say. "Wouldn't it be strange if we saw each other here then?"

Kate says nothing more, and I look over at the pool, then at Kate. Her face is lost in memory. For some reason the thought that comes to me is, if this were a movie, this would be the place for a quiet piano solo. Like the ones on the Windham Hill label they play in the Metronome once in a while. In a few minutes, I am overwhelmed by my own memory, memories, and I resign myself to them. But I do not weep, like Kate. Instead, I smile.

TWENTY-FOUR

At noon the next day I leave the Metronome and take a long walk in today's welcome sun and brisk air to Fat Harry's where Molly said she'd meet me.

We end up spending all afternoon in the place, talking and laughing. I tell her how happy I am. I tell her about my reason-to-get-out-of-bed thing, and how she makes it work so well for me. She tells me about her mother, that she wants me to meet her, and that her mother has a rough time of it every day; I tell her I understand, though I can't, really, not yet. She tells me she once had a cat, when she was a little girl, which her father named Pussy Galore. I tell her about *Goldfinger.*

By dinner, we're hungry enough to eat, so I get a burger, and she has her second one since my arrival, then we leave. We take the streetcar downtown, to the Superdome. It is massive, even in the half-light of the streetlamps. It looks like a great interstellar ship, just landed. The immense boiler stacks belch clouds of steam, and they could easily be the great engines cooling off after a years-long flight from . . . out there, somewhere. Tonight the Dome is dark, deserted, and we walk around the base of it. The night is perfect, impossible to improve. A crystal-clear sky, a full moon, and vigorous, cool air. High above us is an arm of the Milky Way, and there must be billions of stars, cast like a fine dust over the sky.

We walk back to the streetcar stop, and one comes soon. It takes us to Canal, then around to St. Charles, then up toward Lee Circle, and Uptown. All the windows are up, high on their ancient tracks, and a steady artificial breeze fills the car. Molly has her eyes closed, floating in the fresh chill, and I am free to watch her enjoying it.

At Jackson, the car stops. I forgot about Bacchus. I remember hearing John Ritter was supposed to be the king this year, but somehow I can't see it. In the old days, there were *kings,* like Charlton Heston, Phil Harris, Pete Fountain. But John Ritter?

There are thousands of people on the streets tonight, because Bacchus is a genuine spectacle. Crowds maybe ten deep line up to see it, up and down St. Charles, from Lee Circle to Napoleon, and then on Napoleon itself. A sea of faces, each different, each a life separate from the one inches away. It's really something, an experience. Molly and I are pressed together, now warm. Vendors push grocery carts up and down in front of us, selling shiny cellophane wigs and cotton candy. Finally, a police van comes by, signaling the start of the parade.

When the king's float rolls by, John Ritter looks like the god himself, dressed in gold from head to toe, sitting on a throne in front of a huge bust of Bacchus, and bulging papier-mâché arms lift a massive goblet of grape wine to the god's smiling lips. The float stops in front of where Molly and I are standing, and Ritter looks down and sees us waving at him. Next to Molly is a girl, a white girl, with a small black boy on her shoulders so he can see. The boy has the biggest smile on his face I have ever seen. He reminds me of the boy who died. I look back up at Ritter and he nods his head at Molly and tosses down a bunch of purple beads and a handful of sparkling red doubloons. I somehow manage to catch most of them, and I hang a few strands around Molly's neck, then a few around the girl's, then a few around the little boy's. And I give him a few doubloons. He says "Thank you," I can see, but hearing him is next to impossible. Ritter waves to the crowd, and, like on cue, his float moves away, and he showers the streets with handfuls of his red coins. All in all, I decide, a great king.

The crowd roars its appreciation and looks forward to another great year for Bacchus. Never a disappointment, Bacchus, named for the god of wine and spirits and partying, is what Mardi Gras is all about.

At one point, after the first few floats pelt the crowd with gold- and silver-colored doubloons and with dozens and dozens of multicolored beads, the St. Augustine band marches by. The crowd, which knows that St. Aug is the best of the Mardi Gras bands, applauds them. The players, mostly black, must be incredibly happy. And then all at once, the hundreds of people within earshot of the music begin to dance. A wild, almost tribal celebration. *This* is what makes Dixieland.

Eventually, once Bacchus is farther down the avenue, the streetcars begin running again, and we jump back on. We take it the rest of the way uptown, to my grandmother's house. She's out of town, like every year during Mardi Gras, and she has a pool in the backyard.

"You want to go swimming?" I ask.

"No, it's too cold," she says.

I go to the closet and take out a raft. Blown up, it's huge, like a mattress. It takes about ten minutes with the foot pump. When I'm done, Molly kneels down and kisses me hard. Then she stands up and unhooks all the beads and begins to take off her clothes. I follow, and then we put the raft on the water. Very quietly, here in the near-darkness, we lie down, and, floating, we make love.

There are so many things I want to say, but I say none of them. I want nothing to spoil this moment, for her, for me. Afterward, with her, I remember the night in the Quarter, with the woman my father rented me, how for months after, I could taste it in my mouth, I could smell it on my hands, how I was sick. From then until Frankie, and after her, to here, all I have wanted is this. A feeling all through me of . . . I don't know the word. Like, "rightness." It's a feeling like this is the way it was supposed to be when they invented it—making love. Like, no matter what happens now, for the rest of our lives we'll know at least we did *this* right. At the same time, I wonder what it could have felt like if I had done it my way, if I had waited. Was my father right, was it so magical now because I knew what I was doing, how to do it right? I'll never know for sure. But I decide that tonight was everything, complete, and that it would have been, too, the other way, if my path had been a longer one, one littered with waiting.

Silent and very happy, I think it must have been tough for Molly because the last time she did this, I know, it became something horrible, something destructive. She says nothing. I pray that it is because, like me, she simply cannot find the words.

We lie together again, in the damp grass. Molly, smiling, says she has always loved the feel of wet grass, and the smell. I remember hearing that before. The same star dust is over us, like our blanket, and she takes a deep breath. She must be thinking it's beautiful. I tell her she is, and she kisses me. We make love again. She wraps her arms around me, tight, and I marvel that, somehow, we have rung the bell again, like at the spring fair when you hit the register with the mallet and ring the bell. That's it, so perfect, so right.

"What are you thinking?" she asks.

"I'm just thinking how I can't think of any words to tell you what I'm feeling."

"Neither can I. It's so frustrating to be stuck with 'I love you' all the time."

"Try another language," I say.

"What?"

"Another language. *Je t'aime. Te adoro.*"

"Well, me, too."

"*Watashiwa anatao aishitemasu.*"

"Excuse me?"

"*Watashi—*"

"I heard it. What *is* it?"

"Japanese for 'I love you.' "

"Where does a person learn such a thing?"

"I had a friend at school from Japan. He taught me."

"Do you tell all your girls that?"

"No, just you."

"Sure, it takes too long to say it too many times. No one else would have the patience." She laughs. "Say it again."

"*Watashiwa anatao aishitemasu,*" I say slowly.

"Never mind. Let's stick to English, and then we'll know what we mean, okay?"

"Sure . . . Hey, what is it in English again?"

" 'I love you,' remember?"

"Oh, yeah. You tell me."

She takes my face in her hands, making my cheeks warm, and says, "I love you, Deed Smith."

"Ditto, Molly Goldman."

" 'Ditto'? What's that, Portuguese?"

"Yiddish," I say, and Molly laughs as hard as I've ever seen her laugh, and she rolls out of the grass, into the pool. I jump in after her, and though it's cold, we remain embraced against it. We kiss for a long time, and I concentrate on feeling her wet skin against mine, slick. Then we climb back onto the raft and make love again, and after that, dawn comes and the sun colors the sky the perfect shade of blue for the morning after.

TWENTY-FIVE

I wait at the Grill, talking to Michael for a while out front. I haven't seen him in a couple of weeks. He asks if I want something to eat, and I tell him I'm waiting for someone. I tell him Molly, when he asks. After half an hour, though, I get worried, and decide to try and find her. I run over to her house, which is only eight or nine blocks closer to my house from here. I ring the doorbell again and again, but no one answers. A signal comes to mind, weak at first, then stronger and stronger as it becomes obvious that no one is going to open the door: Jason. Sprinting back to the Grill to see if she has come, I see Jason's face before me, wet and pale on the floor, blood on his mouth, steamy in the tiled space, and for once I keep it there because I don't want to see Molly's there instead. When I get back to the Grill, Michael is still out front, now talking to Richard. No sign of Molly.

"Richard," I say, out of breath.

"Hey, Deed," he says.

"You're back, man," says Michael. "What's up?"

"I have to find someone. Richard, I need your car, okay?"

"I'll drive, buddy, just point the way."

We get into the CRX, and I remember the last time I was in it, and what I saw happening on this seat, and that awful girl with no underwear and no teeth, and I have no trouble pushing it away now. I try the bell again when we get back to Molly's, but there's still no answer. With Richard behind me, I go around to the side, looking for an open window, any clue that someone's inside. Then I hear the sound of breaking glass, and I spin around to see that Richard has thrown a brick through a window.

"What are you doing?"

He says, "I see an arm, Deed." He takes off his shirt and wraps it around his fist, then breaks away all the jagged pieces of window glass. The shirt turns quickly red, and he lifts me through the window, and for a split second I remember when I was in the hospital and he gave me the eight ball and said he was off the shit, and how I didn't buy it, but now I think maybe—

—I see the arm at once, and I know it's hers, and my body fills with boiling, liquid panic because I know what I am seeing, and I run into the room, and Molly is there, on the sofa, asleep. I shake her, but she doesn't wake up, so I shake her again. I look around the room, and I spot a brown bottle on the floor, from Hite's Pharmacy. It's empty.

TWENTY-SIX

I stand over her and watch her chest rise and fall; She's alive, I think. She's alive. I can't *stop* thinking it. She is alive. I stand there and hear the words I screamed at Richard, "She's dead! Help me!" and they seem still fresh, only seconds old. And I see Richard running into the room after me, and we listen for a heartbeat, and Richard says he gets something, just like they say on TV, but I think to myself, You're a druggie and you don't know shit about anything—but maybe he *did* hear it, and I have to believe he did. And we get her to the car and tear to the hospital. She's in a treatment room for a long time, and all I can think of is Jane and that boy and her struggle to change the insurance/treatment policy. With that in mind, by some miracle I am able to reach my father and get his insurance information.

Eventually, they wheel her out of the treatment room and into a large elevator with mustard doors, and I follow them up to a room. It's a double, but there's no one in the other bed.

She's alive.

A woman walks into the room. There are black circles

under her eyes, and her eyes are bloodshot, puffy, and one is bruised. She either has been crying or is drunk beyond belief. Looking at her, I choose the second. She does not see me at all, her eyes are on Molly. She puts a hand on Molly's forehead, strokes her hair.

"What did you do to her?" she says, still not looking at me.

"Are you talking to me?" I ask softly.

"What the fuck did you do to her!"

Molly's eyes open, but I say, "Nothing. I *found* her . . ."

"Get out of here. Get your ass out of here," she says to me, one word, carefully, at a time.

Molly's eyes dart around the room, at first wide and confused, then landing on me and sticking. I smile down at her. As far as I can tell, the woman still has not looked up at me, but only out of this side of her face, at my tennis shoes. "I said get out of here—"

"Deed," Molly says. Her voice is weak, light, wispy, but it stops the woman dead in her tracks. "Deed, I'm sorry . . ." An angel's whisper.

I shake my head no, meaning for her not to talk, just to rest.

"Young man, if you're not out of here in ten seconds," she says, again careful, controlled, in single-word shots, "I'll have you thrown out. Do you—"

"Deed," Molly breathes. "Stay with me. Stay with . . ."

"I'm staying," I say, looking at Molly but speaking to the woman.

She grabs a chair and pulls it noisily over to the bed and takes Molly's hand in her own. "Baby," she says, "are you all right? I came as soon as I could. Baby? Can you talk to me?"

Molly's eyes open again and dart around the room, finally landing on the woman next to the bed. "Mother, is . . . ?"

"I'm here, baby, right here."

". . . Daddy . . ."

"No, baby, he's not here. He . . . couldn't come."

"Good. I don't want him here, ever, just you," in wisps, weak. "Just you and Deed," and her eyes close gently.

Molly's mother looks up at me. "Deed?"

I look into her eyes, and I see the years of it, years of the stuff Molly told me about. But it's not there, really, it's like it was put through a strainer, like what's left is the essence of pain. I can't take my eyes away because I see the woman in the photograph my mother showed me. The face is different, but the expression is identical. The heat is the same. I try to find the words for what I'm feeling, which is like the feeling you get when you stand next to a heat lamp. The radiation; the aura, maybe. This woman's aura is like the woman's in the picture. Worse, the woman here is, or was, beautiful. Finally, I say, "Yeah."

She is looking at me now, and I can't shake the feeling, a chill in the face of the heat. "Do you know what happened?"

"No," I say.

"Why are you here?" she asks.

"Why are you?" I say.

Molly's arm rises from the bed and points in my direction. Her fingers are spread out wide, and I take her hand. She squeezes tight, then loosens, then tightens again. I send the signal back, and she repeats it, and I can finally cry because I know she will be fine. I look at her face, and I see tears on her cheeks, and her mouth silently forms the words "I love you" three times.

I look at my watch as the nurses' shift changes. It's 2 A.M.

I remember Molly being awake before, around ten, feeling much better, stronger. In her own word, "alive." When she wakes up, she talks to her mother for a few minutes, and then the woman leaves. We talk about us. I don't ask her anything about the pills because it's over now. If she wants me to know, I figure she'll tell me sometime.

Finally, the nurse goes into a room at the other end of the hall. I quickly tiptoe into Molly's room, praying that the low sound of a late-night rerun covers the click-clack of my motion. I let the door swing shut, and I walk over to her in the dark. I touch her hand, and her eyes open, like she was waiting for me. She smiles.

"I love you" is the first thing she says. She takes my hand and I lift hers to my face. I kiss her palm, then bend over and kiss her mouth.

After a few kisses, she pulls the sheets away from herself.

I take off my shirt, and then my pants, and the rest. I sit down on the bed and untie her gown. I drop it to the floor. In the dark, we lie together. It is quiet here. A band of moonlight lands on her face, and I see her expression, just as it was on the sky ride, as I hoped it was when we made love.

"I'm so sorry," she says after a little while. "I didn't want—"

"Don't say it, don't say anything. It's over now. We're together now. That's all I care about. When I saw you, I didn't know, I didn't think I would survive. For the first time since, I thought about doing it again."

"Please, please never say that. I wish we could just forget about it. I want to be with you, Deed. I want to be alive, with you . . ." She closes her eyes and rests her head against my chest. Her hands move on me gently, smooth on my skin, like mine on hers. We do not make love, but lie in the moonlight, embraced. I have never felt this way. Loving her is no longer a question, will never be again.

When the moonlight washes into dawn, I carefully slip

out of the bed, dress, and watch her sleeping for a while. Before I leave, I lean over her and press my lips to hers, then whisper those words again, and I lay my hand over her heart, to feel the beating. Then I quietly leave, letting the door swing shut, and no one's around to see me. I think about her all the way home. I walk slow so it will take longer, as the sun lifts itself into morning. I can't erase her picture from before my eyes, the picture of that face which in its look tells me everything I want to hear, which in its look injects something magical into me I've never known or imagined before. This time, nothing could ever erase it.

TWENTY-SEVEN

My costume takes about an hour to put on, with all the face paint. This year, I put white all over my face, then black cat stripes shooting out, away from my eyes, three on each side, and a cool red stripe down the center of my face, from my forehead to just beyond the bottom edge of my chin. To set the stuff, I borrow a trick from an old pal: I pat my face with powder, and this sets the makeup, then I splash the powder off with ice-cold water, and then it supposedly won't come off all day, or all night. That's what he said; I guess I'll see.

The plan was to wear black leotards I got from an old friend of Becky's, but it's too cold today, so I go with jeans and a black sweatshirt, and a white Afro wig, which should make me unrecognizable. On top of it all I wear my winter coat, the one with deep pockets. It's Mardi Gras, and if you don't have decent pockets to put the crap in, you've had it.

Reynolds is crazy today, with people wearing costumes in the halls, some staffers, some visitors, it looks like. It's like a cockeyed nightmare, with green ghouls and black cats around every sterilized corner. When I get to Molly's room, her mother and her doctor are there, and both are wide-eyed at my costume. When they're gone, Molly tells me the good news, that she can leave tomorrow.

"They'd let me go now, but they thought it would be better to keep me inside today."

"Yeah, it's freezing outside," I say to her. The weather was iffy for so many days, up and down, that today, of all days, to have it colder than a witch's tit is close to disaster. Having to cope with coats and stuff is going to be a pain in the ass for some, and will surely ruin the day for others.

"Listen, I have an idea," Molly says. "Stay around here and when you get too cold, or if your pockets get full, come back. My mom said she was going to bring some sandwiches and stuff."

"Your mom?"

"It's okay. I told her who you were, all that. She just looks out for me. You know."

"I guess." I'm not too sure that this is going to work out.

"She knows what it's like to face my father every day, so believe me, if I tell her I've found someone who's nice to me, and who makes me happy, then she's with me. And that makes her with you. I promise."

"Are you sure?"

"Trust me. And trust her. She's a nice lady. You'll see."

I want to believe her, I really do. I wonder what it would be like to talk to Molly's mother, to see if she's at all like the way I remember mine, or more to the point, the way I think mine would have been.

Walking over to St. Charles, a couple of blocks away, I decide not to worry about Molly's mother or anything else, to leave it behind me, where most of it belongs anyway.

The morning wind blows hard through the street crowds. Men pushing grocery baskets peddle hot dogs and hot chocolate and coffee and assorted snacks. I get caramel corn.

A group of women comes by, marching to taped music, and they have dozens of strands of "pearls" around their necks. These are the best beads to get, and most of the time, you can get them only from these marching groups, usually in exchange for a kiss. Before they've all gone by, I have managed to trade for a strand of white ones, the best of the best. Must have been the face . . .

A few people walk by and give me the thumbs-up, for my face. One woman even puts her arm around me while her guy takes our picture.

The streets are a mad, passionate party in motion. Hundreds of costumed natives walk by, on their way to the French Quarter. I remember doing that with Jason last year, walking the four or five miles down there. It was the best time we ever had. It wasn't cold last year, so all the costumes were out, and all over the place. Some people in the Quarter, gays mostly, even went nearly nude, with maybe, at most, a jock and pasties—not much more. And the whole time, there were women on the balconies above, stripping off their shirts, swinging their tits over the crowds. Once in a while, some guy full of too many beers would come up behind one and fondle away. And the girl always squealed. There in the Quarter, it was a tight squeeze, with people packed shoulder to shoulder, which made it only warmer. That should go well today, especially.

One year, Jason and I were in a parade, Elks. It was before he and I really became friendly, when he was in with the guys who hated me—or didn't care one way or the other. The Elks parade was like a hundred of these floats, which in this parade are really just decorated flatbed trucks. At Newman, each seventh-grade class has a truck in Elks. The whole year, it's planned and built and the kids are costumed, all by the parents. It's a lot of fun, especially on Mardi Gras day.

When the parade gets downtown, to Canal Street, that's the best moment. It's when the truck you're riding turns the corner onto Canal, and all you see are faces, a sea of faces, a million of them, crammed into every space there is, person after person, all yelling and screaming and dancing and drinking—all the activities of the day. It's like something out of a movie, but bigger, better. No one could stage this big a crowd scene, not even the guy who did all those Bible movies.

And all I tried to do was make eye contact with people, so I could throw them something. Eye contact is essential, if you want to make the best throws to people. Seeing the person get it is the best part of all. Also, it's good if you're on the ground, like today, if you want to catch a lot of stuff. That way, you fill your pockets or bags faster and go home with more beads and doubloons than anyone.

Rex is good this year, even though the wind takes many strands of beads and hangs them on tree branches, and the king—the King of Carnival—looks fairly majestic.

Elks follows Rex, and it's the longest parade, with hours' worth of trucks, one after the other, with no marching bands or anything in between. It's something to see, some of these trucks, built by people, by groups, for a whole year ahead of time, and some of them are so elaborate, with beautiful costumes, sometimes with music and moving parts. Tomorrow, they'll dismantle today's trucks and start planning next year's—if they haven't already. It's a production, that's for sure—the biggest, best free party on the planet.

It takes about an hour to fill my pockets and the capacity of my neck with beads. I push my way through the crowds, losing my place out front at once as the crowd fills it up with a new face. I push past mothers with their children, and peaceful-looking older couples who have seen decades of days like today and who still come, in costumes sometimes, in the spirit all the time. Finally, I reach Reynolds.

Molly is overjoyed at my stash. Her mother is there, and when I say hello, I give her the long strand of "pearls." When she smiles, I see where Molly's smile came from. Today, this morning, she looks cleaned up, really beautiful again. Instantly, I feel better about her, and for just a moment, I wonder what things I do which are just like *my* mother. But only for a moment, because I promised myself to keep it all behind me today.

On the table are tuna-fish sandwiches and hot chocolate and a king cake, with all the Mardi Gras-colored green, gold, and purple sugars still there.

"I got the baby on the first try," says Molly, holding it up. I'd almost forgotten that every king cake has a tiny plastic baby inside, it's been so long since I had one. Molly's expression tells me neither she nor her mother knows the strange comedy of what she has said.

I eat some of everything, starved, because I didn't have time to have breakfast. The king cake is the best I've ever had. I tell Molly's mother, and she says it's from Gambino's, and that doesn't surprise me, because they make the best cakes every year.

All in all, it goes well, even though none of us says much. Mostly, we listen to the sounds of the parade outside. After a little while, I announce that I'm going back out, and that I'll be back soon.

"Deed, I probably won't be here when you get back," Molly's mother says. "Molly tells me you two have a meeting to go to in the morning, and that she'd like you to pick her up here. I just want you to know that I'd like that, too. And"—and I can't quite believe this is the same woman who was here, at the side of this same bed, yesterday—"I want to thank you for getting Molly here so quickly yesterday."

She smiles at me again.

Trying to think of something to say, I manage only to smile back at her. Then I walk over and kiss Molly on the cheek, leaving a black, white, and red stain—the powder-and-water formula has failed—and shake her mother's hand.

"Thanks," I tell her. Then to Molly: "See you later," and then I walk back outside, my coat zipped to my Adam's apple, ready to celebrate like never before.

TWENTY-EIGHT

At nine, I'm at Reynolds to pick Molly up for breakfast. We go to the Grill. It's out of the way, but Molly and I agree it's worth it, and we have a little time to kill. I have two eggs and burnt bacon, because there's nothing like burnt bacon in the morning at the Grill. Molly has a waffle covered with warm maple syrup. Around ten-thirty, I call Kate because we're supposed to stop at her place on the way back to Reynolds for the Board meeting.

There's no answer.

I call Carolyn, in her office, to see if there's been a change in plans. Carolyn says she spoke to Kate last night, and she said that we were going to pick her up around eleven.

Molly and I jump on the streetcar where Carrollton Avenue curves around and becomes St. Charles Avenue, and we take it to Jefferson. We get off and walk back a block to the Octavia. There's no answer when we press Kate's buzzer. A woman with a shopping cart walks up the ramp, and I help her get the cart, filled with bags from Winn-Dixie, to the door. She opens it, and Molly and I follow her inside. Molly walks beside me, up to Kate's apartment, and we knock. Still nothing.

"She probably overslept," Molly says.

"Probably." I wonder momentarily if most suicides are discovered behind closed doors this way. I was, by my father. Molly was, by me, with Richard. And Jason, even though it wasn't a suicide, was—again by me. This, if it's Kate's, I think, is Molly's first. I hope, for us both, it's the last. I try the door, and it's locked, just like I knew it would be. "What time is it?"

"A few minutes after eleven," she says.

I kneel down and lift up the doormat. Nothing. Then I remember Kate saying something about a key in the pot next to the door. I rummage through the leaves at the bottom. Nothing. Then I remember where my grandmother used to keep the key to her house, in a pot like this, but at the edge. So I run my fingers around the edges until they come to a small manila envelope. Bingo. Inside is the key.

Everything is quiet, once we are inside the dark space of the apartment. On the table in the living room is the tea set Kate used when I was here before. There's a single teacup with a sip or two of tea left at the bottom.

"I don't think she's here," Molly says. "It's so quiet."

"Wait a second. Let's see," I say. "The bedroom's this way." We go down a short corridor, then make a right. The bedroom door is closed, but not locked. I turn the knob and walk in. The shades are pulled shut, so when I open the door, I let a little of the hallway light into the pitch room. Just enough for me to see Kate, asleep on the bed.

"Kate?" Molly says. She walks over and gently shakes Kate's shoulder. But Kate doesn't move, doesn't stir. "Kate?"

"Molly, stop," I say.

"Kate, wake up," a little more urgent.

"Molly, stop. Come here." On the desk is a pile of

papers. It's an essay, handwritten in a shaky script, about three pages long, paper-clipped. I pick it up and read the first few lines. "When I volunteered to speak to you . . ." it says.

Molly is beside me now. I put the papers down and look back at Kate. Molly takes my hand. "She's dead, isn't she?"

She could be asleep. Her face is so peaceful. That sunny face. It's almost smiling. Oh God, I think. I breathe deep. Then, absently: "Yeah."

It was ninth grade the last time I felt this feeling, like there's a hole in me somewhere, sucking every other part of me dangerously close to its edge.

It was a Monday afternoon, and I was in my room watching after-school TV, and Becky was out bike riding. She screamed, that was when I knew something was wrong. I ran outside and she was in front, looking into the gutter. Lying there was Mary, stiff.

We'd had her since I was two. Our mom found her at a birthday party and put her in the cake box. We named her Mary Poppins after the movie; it was the first movie Becky ever saw.

Mary was the best cat there was. An alley, she was a grand old lady from the start, very chic, commanding her own position in the house. Feather-soft gray and white, with sky-blue eyes, and the most incredible "meow" you ever heard. She would claw-climb straight up our dad's pants and shirt, all the way to his shoulders, then perch there, perfectly balanced, Queen of the Mountain. She would come running whenever Mom sang something, anything, from *South Pacific.* And on the days when my dad and I would come back from a breakfast at the Grill, Mary would be curled up in Mom's lap, out on the patio. Mary was family.

Now dead.

I couldn't take my eyes away for a second, but then I went inside and called Dad. His voice was cracked, and I thought he was crying again, for the then second time in my life, but I couldn't be sure. I told him I wanted to bury her in the yard.

I found his old shovel and went out to her. I scooped her up and carried her to the back. I laid her on an old Holiday Inn towel. She was already stiff, but there was no blood. It was weird. There were none of the signs of death, like broken bones, or a crushed body; nothing. She looked just like she always did when she was asleep in the sun on the sill in the kitchen, her gray-and-white coat shiny in the dusty afternoon glare.

Then I began to dig through the grass and dirt. It was easy after the first few shovels were away, and I dug until I was going straight down.

When I began to pick up the corners of the towel, Lesley came out. I figured Dad had called her. Lesley and her husband used to have a Newfoundland, who died. So she knew.

She asked me if I was okay, and I said I thought so. Still, she put her arms around me for a second, and it was good to feel her touch, and her understanding. Becky, her eyes red and her hair messed up, came out. We all lifted Mary into the hole. We said a few prayers and hugged each other.

Becky and Lesley went in after the first shovelful of dirt was put back into the hole, and I filled it up the rest of the way. When I was done, I turned around and saw my grandmother standing there.

"Your father rang me," she said.

I knew she didn't understand this ceremony for a cat, not at all. But she said nothing about it. I dropped the shovel and went to her and she held me tight, like my mom used to do. I imagined her holding my mom like this a long time ago. Finally, I began to weep, and it came with such a force that I shook. Yet we held on.

Molly and I arrive at the hospital in the back of Kate's ambulance. We enter through the Emergency Room, where I first saw Jane, where I saw the little black boy just before he died. We walk to the elevators and follow the directions to the Executive Offices. When we get there, a red-haired woman with a man's face opens the door for us. Inside a large room are many men in dark suits, and a few women, and Carolyn and Jane. No one says anything. I avoid Carolyn's eyes, looking instead at the paintings of old men on the dark wood walls. There is one large window, similar to the one in Carolyn's office, but we're higher here, and through it I can see the city, selfishly involved in its own problems and celebrations, not even slightly concerned about this room, or us. Or our futures. There are two empty seats at the table. Molly and I walk to them, and I look at her in time to see her blink away her tears for Kate. I take her hand, and we squeeze our signal. I look down at the sheets of paper we found in Kate's apartment. Molly pulls out one of the heavy chairs with a red leather seat, and sits. I look at her there for a second, then walk to a tiny podium at the head of the long wooden table. I carefully place the papers down, and look at Carolyn.

"I'm sorry we're late," I say. My voice is louder than I geared it to be; the suddenness of the sound makes it seem much louder than it is. I feel every ounce of energy in this room focused on me. It is the heaviest of energy, and it's a burden I want to be quickly rid of.

"We were at Kate's."

I see Carolyn's eyes asking why, but her mouth says nothing.

Standing there, I am suddenly unable to speak. I move my mouth open and closed, hoping it will get my throat on the ball, but still there is silence. The air conditioner switches on, blasting sheets of icy air into the room. Typically, after yesterday's freeze, it's a warm winter day today. I scratch an itch on my forehead, and my finger comes away damp with sweat.

Molly looks over the men and women at the table and says to us all, "Kate James died in her sleep last night."

At once, all the faces turn to Molly, and Carolyn begins to weep, her fists pressed against her tightly closed eyes. Molly's face becomes streaked with tears again. I become even warmer and more uncomfortable, if that's possible, and I feel a tear of sweat run down my back. Now, finally, I have a chance to cry, and I remember Mary Poppins, how I'd held it in until I just couldn't any longer. It feels good, oddly, to be totally open to the men and women who never knew Kate. Only momentarily do I imagine what they could be thinking of our display.

Then Molly says, "We found her while we were on our way here. We called an ambulance, and she's downstairs. In her apartment, we found the papers Deed has, the words she was going to say to you today."

Molly looks at me, and I manage an "Uh," which tells me I can speak now. "This," I say slowly, "is what Kate wrote." I pause, thinking, Read it the way Kate would have, slowly and with her power.

" 'When I volunteered to speak to you today, I had no idea it would be so difficult. For many days, I have been thinking about what I wanted to say to you. I am eighty-four years old, and I have neither written anything of this kind nor addressed any group, so you must forgive me for my awkwardness.

" 'I came to the Suicide Counseling Group one year

ago. At the age of eighty-three, I tried to drown myself. I would like to tell you why.

" 'When I was eighty, my husband passed away. Ben was a year older than I was, and when he died, we had been married sixty years. We had one daughter, who lives in New York with her husband and our grandchildren. Ben was the first.

" 'After his death, I mourned my husband, but I did not mourn for too long. Just as he would have wished, I put my life back in order and went on with it. But soon, one by one, over the next three years, I lost all my friends. Mostly to cancer. As soon as I was done mourning for one, another would go, until the last, Lucy, one of my dearest friends.

" 'When Lucy died, there was nothing left. No friends, nothing to do or see, no one to talk to the way we used to. Nothing left to feel, but pain. I wonder if any of you can know what it is like to feel only pain. What it is like to have nothing to look forward to, day after day. To spend your life with dear friends, and then to lose all of them. To have a wonderful life, then to be left alone with a fading memory.

" 'These were my thoughts when I tried to kill myself.

" 'But when I was under that water, I saw that there was a reason to live, after all, and I fought my way back up, back to the air, back to life.

" 'I didn't climb out of that pool a new woman. It took me a year to be new again, thanks to Carolyn Moore. She was a dear friend to an old woman who desperately needed her in order to survive. But Carolyn was not only my friend. She was also my doctor. She guided the way back to living. She offered advice. She opened the door and walked through it right beside me. She *listened* to me. I could not have done it without her. But for her, I would not be here.

" 'Still, I am not the only such "friend." Standing up here with me are three others. Jane Weller, you know. As a former member of this Board, she fought to save lives. She believed that certain policies at Reynolds Center were wrong. She fought to change them, and she consulted Carolyn Moore in order to come to terms with the conflict she felt between her morals and her work at this hospital. When she resigned, this hospital lost one of its most qualified and compassionate physicians. When she left her seat on this Board, you lost the best means of communication between this room and the hospital it controls.

" 'Deed Smith is here.' " I have to stop reading. I can almost hear Kate's own voice, saying my name, saying the sentence again, for me alone to hear. Go on, I think. Read. Read it the way Kate would.

" 'Deed Smith is here,' " I continue. " 'He is a new friend, and the newest member of our group. He is eighteen, and he is very bright. He attempted suicide recently. When I met him here at Reynolds Center, he was just recovering. Today he is not the boy I met, no longer sad and suspicious. He is now an adult. He opened the door and walked through it the wrong way. Carolyn Moore held his hand and walked him back, as we all did. She has helped him immeasurably.

" 'Next to Deed is Molly Goldman . . .' "

I stop reading again and look up at the air, at nothing, really, perhaps searching for an image of Kate to match the voice I hear now. My eyes dart nervously around the room, then land on Molly. The room is silent. I try to smile, though I know the one I manage is minimal. Her cheeks glow with tears. I do not look away, I know she needs me to be here, as I need her. After a moment, she looks down at the table, and I continue.

" 'Next to Deed is Molly Goldman. She has been a member of our group the longest, for more than six years.

Molly came to the Suicide Counseling Group because she felt a need to end her life, yet knew she did not really want to. Molly has not attempted suicide in all this time.' "

I stop now, realizing for the first time that it has been four impossible days since I last saw Kate—at the zoo, I think. No one told her about Molly, and standing here, I decide that was good; somehow, in all the confusion, Kate was spared the knowledge. So, I realize, were Carolyn and Jane.

After a moment's pause, I go on. " 'In the past year, Molly has become a beautiful woman, one I would be proud to have as my granddaughter. In a way, she is, and I think she feels the same. Her progress is also immeasurable, thanks to Carolyn Moore.

" 'Before you, then, are four people who need more than anything to be loved. Who need to know that someone is there, not just someone who is put there, but someone who *feels.*

" 'For each of us, there are many, many others who are not here. Some, because their attempts to kill themselves were not stopped in time. Others, because they have not been fortunate enough to find this program. Many of those may even have attempted suicide a second time, and succeeded. One of these, Lynn Waters, did. She was our dear friend, and we miss her.

" 'To remove the Suicide Counseling Group is to remove our only chance. The one telephone number we have to dial where we know we will find a voice, a real voice, not one that may for all its feeling be a recording. For people such as we four, to know that number is vital. Our trust that someone will answer is a trust we have in the same way as the one which tells us who we are. It is something we *know.*

" 'None of us believes the group can disappear without leaving a hole in the needs of everyone in this city. But what may be beneficial as an amendment to the present program is a new design, so that the group is populated by those who find they need our help *before* they attempt suicide. These are the people the Suicide Counseling Group was really formed to help. Treating attempters must, however, remain as certainly nothing less than a secondary function.

" 'Coming here meant different things to each of us, at the beginning. For me, it was treatment, plain and simple. I had a problem. But then I was surprised. I got to know Carolyn, and the others. She became my new friend. I saw the kind of special person she is. For all of us here, I know I can say she is one of a kind. Her treatment is unique. And it's not always easy. She can be rough sometimes. But in her roughness, she *cares.* She feels. When we meet as a group once a week, we create the ultimate healing place, one built on love. There is no healthier place I know. I cannot imagine the group not being here for me, and I cannot imagine not being here for them.

" 'Do you even know how our group works? I'll tell you, quickly. We exchange addresses and telephone numbers. With these we exchange a trust. It isn't anything we say or sign, but an understanding. Each of us meets with Carolyn at least once a week, and most of the time more often, and once every week we meet as a group.

" 'What do we discuss? Anything at all. We talk. We sing. We fight. We dream. Carolyn is not a moderator, but a participant. She does not separate herself, but immerses herself, opening herself up as wide as we all do, trusting us as we trust her, and each other.' " For a second, I remember the day in her office, near the window . . .

" 'It is a unique experience. I think before you remove Dr. Moore or this program, you should experience a group session. You should become a part of our society as we are desperately trying to become again a part of yours. *Then* you should think about what you feel you need to do.

" 'I say, feel. That's all: feel. It's an extraordinary thing, feeling. I've been doing it for eighty-four years now. I lived a long life of joy and pain and sorrow. We each have our share. And I am still living it. And for as long as I live, I will know that one night, I tried to end my life. But I survived. Thanks to the love of one woman and a small group of friends.

" ' I think you will enjoy what it means to feel. You will laugh, you will cry, and sometimes you will be hurt. And what a waste it would be *not* to! If you get hurt, I say deal with the pain and go on from there. Don't run away from it. Have the courage to feel, and never lose it. Feel everything. I can tell you, it's worth it all, all the pain, for what we get from the joy, from just being alive. The price we pay in sorrow is worth what we get in happiness. Have the courage to *live*, as I did, as we all have, as we all will.' "

A day later, we are all brought face to face again by Kate's funeral.

Everything is harder now, taking much more effort, almost like the thing that kept us all going is gone. Still, there is a distinct lump in my throat, not the kind they talk about in sad movies, but a throbbing stubbornness against crying, which has come as a revolt against my need to let it go, because if I let it go, I fear I may never get it back again. I keep my tongue and my emotions in control —and the ache it all forms in my throat is the price I pay.

Jason, I discover, is in my thoughts constantly, like a dull humming sensation that I can't switch off. It's not irritating, really—just there. Enough to let me know. Funny, the hum even *acts* like Jase, now that I think about it. Jason's funeral was only a few weeks ago. How it hurt me to miss it. How it twisted my insides to realize I was so caught up in my own life that I—that I forgot his death. Even for just a moment.

We all stand around the hole in the earth. Kate's box is suspended over it. Each hand is holding another.

There are not too many of us here on this cold, sunny afternoon. Jane and Carolyn and Molly, of course. Also a woman who looks so much like Kate, I shiver when I see her. She stands with a man who must be her husband, and three children. The woman must be Kate's daughter from New York City. Several doctors and nurses are here, I guess the ones who took care of her whenever she was in Reynolds for her tests. Finally, my father is here.

At first, I don't understand it. Then, by the time we all gather at the gravesite, my hand locked in his, I decide that I don't need to understand this. It's enough that he's here with me—for me.

After the rabbi steps aside, it's my turn. I have been asked to say something about this woman we all loved.

All the eyes here turn from Kate's box, with lengths of flowers draped over it, to me. This time, I am not nervous. Oddly, it seems right to be here now, and after days of struggling with what to say, suddenly I know.

Before I begin to talk, though, I think once more of Jason. I make these few seconds my funeral for him. I love you still, I think to him. I will never forget you, and what you did for me without even knowing it. I will always miss you. And I will not lose what we had. Our bond, made of lightning and flying rain, is as strong as ever. Though it'll be a long while, I'll be with you again someday. Remember everything . . . and . . . wait for me.

"My friend Kate," I begin, feeling tears for my two friends already on my face, "was, I don't know, very special. But more than just special. She was a gift, and the way she touched all of us was *her* gift. Of course, she touched us all in different ways, but I think each way had one part in common with the others, and that was the youth of her spirit, the youth in her eyes. In a woman Kate's age, it must have been wonderful to feel so young. I don't think there was anything Kate thought she couldn't do, I don't think there was anything she— No, I'm sorry. There *was* one thing Kate was afraid of. Being alone. Kate was a woman who needed other people around her, all the time. It was her love for them which made her that way. Kate was a woman who met the world with love, and the way she felt about everyone she met—that's what made her so special to us. Even though she's gone now, and even though we feel a loss, we haven't lost. We have only gained from knowing Kate. She asked for nothing in return, but we gave her what she wanted most, our love. Looking around, I see no one Kate's own age. Now, that could be because there's no one left; Kate once told me that all her best friends were dead. But I think it's a tribute that we are all here for her today. I'm here because she had the fairly unique ability to talk to me on my own level, not as a son or as a boy she knew—but as a friend, as an equal. I think that because her family lived out of New Orleans, Kate longed for a new group of people to care for. Her ability to communicate with young people says a lot about the kind of woman she was, about what she wanted. Though I didn't know Kate very long, we were very good friends, and I knew her well, and there's one thing I know for sure about her. What I know she wanted, was not to live forever, but to always have her friends and a full life all around her while she was alive. She became a young person every time she met someone new to love. She once told me that people could be alive forever if their achievements lived on, shining bright after their deaths. I know that I will keep Kate alive as long as I'm alive—in my mind, in my eyes and ears, and mostly, in my heart."

There is silence, then, for a few moments, until a slight breeze causes the trees to whisper their own benediction.

Not long after, in fact just three days, the three of us meet in Carolyn's office. Right off the bat, Carolyn tells Molly and me that the Board hasn't made a final decision yet, though she thinks they're planning to redesign the program, to get it into people's heads and make it available *before* the suicide attempt. She uses the phrase "public awareness," and we all agree that sounds like the best solution.

We are seated in a circle on the floor in her office. Through the window, the city is alive below, even on this dark, wet day. A gray quilt hangs depressingly over the city, dulling even the stark whiteness of the Superdome, and there's a sharp wind that whistles around the corner of the building. The weather hasn't let up since the night of the funeral. Outside, the strength of the wind easily convinces the trees to bend, as if to worship; other trees are more resistant, only shaking in their roots. Maybe they're afraid of the future.

Molly and I have finally talked about her suicide attempt. She knows she has to come to grips with it, and this is where she has to do it. Facing it here will release her from the guilt she says she feels; we both know that. I told her that she feels she's been dishonest with them, and with Kate.

"And with myself," she said the other day.

"I want to start today," she says now.

"Okay," says Carolyn.

"Can I talk for a little while? Alone? And can y'all just listen to me?"

"Sure. That's okay."

"Okay. I . . . I don't know how to do this," she says. Her eyes are on me, then off me, then on again. I know she's nervous, and that she knows she has to do this. For herself. Now. "I have to tell you something I haven't told you, and it's going to hurt maybe all of us." She looks at Carolyn. "It may threaten the group."

"It's all right, Molly," says Carolyn. She leans forward and covers Molly's hand with her own.

Molly looks at the hands, then swallows hard. She says, "Right before Mardi Gras, I tried to commit suicide."

The first thing I see is Carolyn's hand uncovering Molly's. And that's the moment I decide—or, really, *know*—that this is my last session with Carolyn, no matter what. It's a flash of thought that I decide to hold on to, that's what it is.

"For real," Molly says. There is only a slight pause, when Molly sees Carolyn's hand move away. "I was alone, and I took a bottle of pills. I did it because . . . because I had to. It was the only way out. It was the only way away from the screaming, from the blood. The dreams."

"What dreams?"

"There was a dream. A . . . a rape. It was like a white-hot poker inside me . . . there, burning me away to nothing. And the blood, like before, it wouldn't stop, nothing could stop it. And I didn't have eyes anymore . . ."

We all sit there, silent, waiting. The wind tries to make the building bend like the lesser trees, but the building answers it only with the sounds of old age. Soon, even more powerful, the wind whistles, perhaps calling for reinforcements.

"I kept thinking about before, about the abortion, the hanger. And part of me saw how right you were"—she looks straight at Carolyn—"to think it was a suicide attempt. I guess . . . I guess it was, sort of. Only I didn't know it. I . . . didn't want to know it."

Molly struggles on with it for a while longer, finally telling us that the reason for this second attempt was the memory—the thoughts and feelings she'd kept pent up inside for so many years, released by making love to me. She stressed that it was the sex, the *act* of it, that brought it up again. Little by little, it gets easier for her to talk about it. Her voice goes back to normal, losing the tight, grainy sound it's had for a week. It's like her throat finally lets it all out, this shit that's been building and building since that afternoon. Soon, she even sees that we all begin to understand, and that we are, so far, surviving this confession. Still, I am surprised at Carolyn's moving her hand at that moment, when Molly surely needed it there the most. The fact that Molly continues with it, despite Carolyn, tells me how strong this confession has made her already. In her eyes, I can see she is glad she went through with it.

"But you know, there's one thing. I still don't know what my—what? trigger?—trigger is, but maybe it's one that doesn't have words. And there's something else, too. After I swallowed the pills, part of me regretted it. The part that loves being alive, the part that loves you, Deed. By then, I guess, the other part, the part that had the dreams, the part that needs to get away from the screaming, that part was in control. That part wanted to escape, to die, more than the other part wanted to live."

Molly looks at me now, and I smile a little for her.

No one says anything.

Then I say, "It was the same with me." I look at both of them. "It was the same with me. There was a part that wanted to live . . . and a part that needed to die. And for me, needs outweigh wants. Somewhere inside me, I was revolting against my whole life, all at once. Like Kate said, I was trying to recover from being hit by that damned truck. On one hand, I kept remembering the good things, but on the other, I kept seeing the . . . like the night I walked into the living room and found my father fucking

Frankie on the floor, and the look in his eyes when he saw me there—and how all I wanted to see was *my* eyes, so I could maybe deal with what I saw in them, but I couldn't . . ."

Molly begins to nod.

". . . I could only feel them, burning. I kept seeing Jason's bloated face, and Chip's OD'd face, and how now that they were dead, I was alone again. And I didn't want to be—couldn't be—back there again, like before. The fight to get away from there had been too long, too hard; to be back there would have . . . killed me. I saved it the trouble. Or I tried to. I couldn't be—wouldn't be—alone again, not like before."

I realize it sounds a lot like Kate. She couldn't bear being alone, either. How many gifts would she give to me, how many ways to keep her alive?

"I used to go fishing with my father," I find myself saying. "In the boat, I used to play with the eyes of the dead fish. They were shiny and smooth, the eyes, and if you pushed them, they would roll around in their sockets. In the sun, though, they dried out . . . I used to look at people's eyes. It's neat, if you really look, because they look like marbles, sort of. Like, if you took a marble and shattered it inside, all the cracks and lines and edges, that's what an eye looks like. But fish eyes, they aren't like that. They don't look cracked. It's like they're all the same. Sometimes I think the reason we all see the world differently is because of the cracks in our eyes. Each one of us has different cracks, and the cracks determine the way the world looks to each of us. The funny part is that they also determine the way we see ourselves. Almost like, before we're born, our eyes are like a fish's—smooth, clean, unbroken. But as soon as we're born, or maybe just before, something inside us knows what's to come, how tough it is out here, how hard it is just to live, sometimes. And that something, that force, whatever it is, tries to help us, and it shatters our eyes, our . . . our perceptions, forever. It's that shattering that makes us live and see things the way we do. And . . . lets us."

For a quiet moment, we sit there in our places. Even the wind has stilled itself.

"It's just that some of us, some people's eyes are shattered later. And that's when we're really born. Finally."

TWENTY-NINE

Two months later, on the most beautiful April morning we have ever seen, I go with Molly to the seal pool at the zoo. There's still no water, there are no seals. But there is a past, the past I remembered the last time I was here, and there is a future. A future for me, with Molly.

I think of Kate's words, the ones she spoke to me many, many days ago, the ones about achievements. I hear her again, saying, ". . . life is like a sun. We do things, we feel things, we're even warm. We're part of everything. But all that's left after we die is what we did, our achievements, our past . . ."

I think about what the achievements will be of Kate's sun, and then I remember that when I first saw her, the sun was what I thought of. I think of her face now, again and again, all its different expressions. The way there were so many wrinkles, and the way they lifted and disappeared when she smiled. The color of the sky in her eyes. Her golden hair, never quite as neat as she would have liked. I know now that when we die, we must make sure we shine for as long as we can, after. I think that Kate will shine for a very long time, that her sun will burn very bright, and I smile. Molly asks me what I'm thinking about, and I tell her it's Kate. She says she knows. But I don't think she does. She will when I tell her. In the weeks since Kate's funeral, since that last day at Carolyn's, Molly's face has brightened. I can't help thinking now that we are all connected in important ways, that each of us helps the other get back into living, and that it's a constant thing, all of it, constant.

We walk around the seal pool once more, and somehow the sky is wiped in pastels of pink and orange. I can't erase Kate's face from before me, or her voice from inside my ears. I know that I won't try to erase them or anything else, ever again, that I won't let them be eclipsed. I want to use all the images, to use their strength, their power, so that somehow, Jason's, and Chip's, and Kate's, and my mom's suns will all burn in me.

As we leave, I take Molly's hand. Somewhere behind me, I can still hear seals barking at feeding time, me in my grandmother's arms.